WORTS 'N' ALL

Stewart MacInnes

WORTS 'N' ALL

DOUBLE DRAGON

Foreword

Worts 'n' All is a collection of short stories I've written over the years; more than I care to say. Some of the stories I wrote with a friend or two which brings back memories of evenings discussing ideas of plots and characters. A lot of these stories were published in small press magazines which were once in abundance in the days before the internet. One by one though these small press magazines ceased publication and to my knowledge none of the ones I subscribed to exist today.

The stories are a mixed bunch. Ghosts, love, adventure, social injustices and environmental concerns are all featured in this book but there's also humorous stories and a few which are just plain silly.

I had to decide what order the stories should be in. I could have blocked each type together or I could have separated the ones I wrote by myself from those written with friends. I decided though to arrange each story in alphabetical order which I concluded was not only the simplest thing to do but is as a good an order as any.

This book of short stories are ideal reading for when you've got five minutes or so to spare as they can be read from start to finish in a short space of time.

Contents

One Hell Of A Day
The Priceless Book
The Red Door *
Roger's Match **
Rufus
The Runabout **
Snapshot *
Stolen Love
The Stranger **
Under The Bright Blue Sky **
Utopia Island
Wedding Bells
When A Child Is Born
When I Propose *
When The Screaming Stops **
1st February '93

All stories written by Stewart MacInnes except:
*Written by Stewart MacInnes and Bob Dark *
Written by Stewart MacInnes, Bob Dark and
*Graham Radband ***

After The Event

"Tell you what, I live a few minutes from the station, give me a ring when you arrive."

Good idea, I thought. Wrong! No telephones in the station and the two outside didn't work.

One of them had a jammed coin in the slot. Try as I may nothing was going to shift it. I couldn't force the coin through the slot or pull it out. The wretched thing had me beaten. I reckon there's a little man in there making sure the coin stays stuck. The other phone just simply spat my money out. As the coins slipped down the eject tube, I could have sworn they were laughing at me. Ten or twenty pence pieces, it didn't matter, the phone wouldn't take any of them. It's good to talk - if you get the chance.

I'd felt uneasy about the whole thing from the start; my stomach had left me with an uncomfortable feeling all day. Maybe it was just the fact I was travelling to London. The City had that effect on me, always made me feel apprehensive, just the thought of being there.

What was I doing anyway? I could have stayed at home and watched *Kavanagh* on TV. Instead I was trying to find a phone box so that I could ring my blind date. What was I worried about? I'd set the video and, what the heck, nothing ventured nothing gained so they say.

I'd previously caught a tube train, which crawled along to endless eternity. The sky was dark. Through the carriage window I watched the flickers of orange and white street lights forming unusual but interesting shapes as the train rolled slowly onwards. Then the carriage's internal lights began to flicker on and off as the train appeared to be bouncing along the track. I thought it was going to bounce off at any moment. For a while, I didn't think we were going to make it.

I listened to a conversation between an Australian couple which helped to take my mind off the journey. The man had a patch over his eye, but all the same, he looked nothing like a pirate. His lady companion looked and sounded very concerned, about what, I was unable to grasp. He kept telling her he would do the talking and sort it out. Sort what out? I was nosey and I wanted to know. Yet despite this, when the train arrived at my stop, I was glad to get off.

So there I was. Walking further and further from the station trying to find a phone box that worked. Finally I came across one.

I dialled my date's number. Nothing happened. I came over all in a flush. Had I written her number down incorrectly? I dialed again. This time I got through.

"I'm outside the Abbott Hotel."

"I don't know where that is."

"I'll walk back to the station and wait for you there."

I marched back up the road passing one fast food place after another. How do they all stay in business? Doesn't anyone cook their own food around here? The stench from some of these places did nothing to settle my stomach. It's amazing what some people will eat these days.

I waited outside the station for my date. I saw a young lady walk towards me. I knew it must be her. She fitted the description. Long blonde hair. About five foot three.

Before I could make contact she was confronted by the Australian couple. I watched them enter a coffee bar and through cigarette smoke I could see that they were arguing. I thought about going inside but I came to the conclusion it was none of my business.

I never made contact with her again and, I must admit, I'd almost forgotten about her but this morning I saw her picture in the paper. She's been accused of smuggling Australian artefact. She says she's innocent and I believe her. I should have gone into that coffee bar and helped her. Still, it's easy to be wise after the event.

Her case comes up tomorrow but the evidence against her is very flimsy. In fact, Kavanagh won't be needed for this one. I'll be there to lend moral support but she won't know who I am of course.

After she's acquitted I'll wait outside the court for her. Maybe then, we'll get to have a cup coffee.

All Those Years Ago

The ten-thirty train from London brought a handsome young man, seeking to avoid the London blitz, to the small village of Wint. You walked up the high street and stepped into the Green Dragon with that cheeky grin on your face. As fate would have it I was helping the landlord out that day - pulling pints behind the bar.

The old lady who sat in the corner near the door soon latched onto you. With a shawl which hung from her shoulders like ill-fitted curtains, her bony fingers that clenched her glass of stout, she amused you with yarns and folklore. No sooner had she finished telling one tale, she would hold out her glass at arms length, you dutifully obliged her with more stout. Had I not come to your rescue she would have skinned you down to your last penny.

I think you'd taken an instant shine to me, at least I'd hoped as much, I thought you were gorgeous. I had beautiful dark hair and my rosy cheeks were a sight to behold you teased.

Your eyes lit up like London's neon lights when I mentioned Metcalf Farm. It was just what you were looking for, ideal for your needs. A small farm but there was an abundance of vegetables and other crops, all ready to be picked.

You'd talked me into it, after all, we needed some help on the farm and when I'd finished my stint behind the bar we were on our way. The rain had stopped but it had left behind a sea of puddles, so deep, it felt as if we were walking on water. You were so excited, you could have walked across a lake and never noticed.

Do you remember the day we declared our love? I still have vivid memories of you getting down on one knee and as a token of your love you placed a red rose in my hand. I've never felt so alive as I was that night; we could have been the only people on Earth and it wouldn't have mattered. Graciously you asked me to be your wife, the moonlight's approval shone brighter than noonday.

We would be married in St. Peters Church that stood so pretty on Beacon Hill. But then came your call-up papers. We knew they would come. I'd always hoped they wouldn't.

We decided to postpone our wedding plans until after the war. You said it wouldn't be right to begin married life with yourself away most of the time. You promised the war would soon be over and we'd settle down to have a family.

Whenever you went away I prayed for you, night and day, asking God to keep you safe. Bravely you went into battle with the troops just a few months before the war ended in 1945. All those years ago.

News came of your death. My heart died with it. I kept praying for a miracle, hoping you'd come home with that cheeky grin on your face. But you never came back.

I met my husband, Peter, a year after the war ended and we married in 1947. Peter was a very famous musician in those days, known throughout Europe, I believe. I expect you read about our wedding in the newspapers.

I'm very lucky to have such a wonderful family. I have two lovely daughters - Elizabeth and Julia. Four grandchildren - Mark, Andrew, Kate and Anne. My eldest, Elizabeth, is married to David and Michael is Julia's husband. Collectively they run Metcalf Farm and I lend a hand whenever I can.

I got quite a shock when I read about you in the magazine. You've become something of a celebrity I understand. I recognised you in the picture instantly. Those lovely blue eyes. Your hair is old and grey now, but those good looks and that cheeky grin are unmistakeable.

My prayers were answered - you didn't die on the battlefield. Instead you were so badly injured you spent two years in France before you were well enough to return to England.

I'm sorry to hear that your wife died three years ago - Peter passed away around that time too. I've never forgotten you, you've always been in my heart. Dare I write and ask an old soldier to take another trip on the ten-thirty from London? Fifty years on, St. Peters Church still stands pretty on Beacon Hill.

Aunt Nellie's Cupboard

I watched as the furniture removal van sped off down the road taking with it what remained of Aunt Nellie's household contents. Although most of the stuff was worn and somewhat shabby, no doubt the YMCA would find a good home for it all.

Her house was empty now. Nothing else remained save the dust particles that covered the fixtures and fittings. She'd left just enough money to take care of her last affairs. Everything had been accounted for right down to the last penny, as precise and correct as Aunt Nellie herself.

When I was a child my mother used to leave me with Aunt Nelly every Wednesday morning whilst she went shopping down at the market. I used to play quietly with my Lego, long before the invention of Duplo, until my mother returned with bags full of fruit and vegetables. As payment for baby sitting she would always bring back a big yellow melon for Aunt Nellie.

As I stood in her front bedroom I was determined and anxious to take one more look. It seemed so much different from my childhood, but as I gazed the room my eyes became fixed on Aunt Nellie's Cupboard.

Even as a young child that cupboard held such wondrous mysteries before me. She always kept it locked and although I never got to see what was inside, my curiosity had never waned.

"What's kept in here is not for the eyes of one so young," she used to say.

Those words are very clear to me now but as an infant I never understood much of what she said. It never occurred to her that my vocabulary was very limited and that, "don't touch," "good boy," or "dinner's ready," was about as much as I could comprehend.

She'd never married and as a consequence had no understanding of children at all. She could never appreciate why I never drank the cup of teas she used to make for me or how I could occupy my mind for so long playing with my Lego. I was actually very good at making things with it, took a lot of skill, these days children have it too easy playing with their oversized Duplo.

I can remember the day when I'd just finished building a house and I could hear voices coming from Aunt Nellie's Cupboard. I thought something was hissing at me earlier but that had failed to grab my attention.

"Let me out, let me out, let me out," the voice kept crying.

I put down my Lego. I moved closer to the cupboard and put my ear to it.

"I can't get out, someone's locked me in, please help me," the desperate voice kept repeating.

17

I tried to communicate but either they didn't understand or they couldn't hear me speak. As I listened intently to its cries for help I began to imagine who might be trapped in the cupboard. A lost, defenceless little girl came to mind. She would have curly red hair with matching freckles that covered her nose and chubby cheeks.

The cupboard was locked as usual. Aunt Nellie had the only key and she was downstairs baking a chocolate cake having left her instructions that she wasn't to be disturbed.

"Aunt Nellie - cupboard," I shouted, but my cries for help were unanswered.

The little girl's cry was like an animal's in pain so I decided to negotiate the stairs and disobey Aunt Nellie's orders. Like an old person frail on their feet, I would normally keep my hand held firmly on the banister whilst taking each step slowly and deliberately until I'd reached the ground floor. This time I imagined I was in a toboggan race. Bravely I sat my bottom on the top stair and slid all the way down. I then rushed into Aunt Nellie's kitchen oblivious to the repercussions.

"Aunt Nellie - cupboard," I pleaded.

"What is it, Donald?" she asked impatiently.

She always called me Donald. I was Donny to everyone else but she insisted on being formal. Mum and Dad only called me Donald when I'd done something wrong. I would then close my eyes and embrace myself for a smack across the legs. But

18

in Aunt Nellie's case I never had prior warning for the whack I was going to get.

Against the odds I managed to persuade her to abandon her chocolate cake for a while and to go up stairs. Irritated, she quickly made her way up, leaving me to negotiate each step by myself. Crawling on my hands and knees I conquered Everest to make it back to the front bedroom.

"Now what is it, Donald?" she shouted.

I pointed to the cupboard. She looked at me very cross.

"I haven't time to play games, Donald. What's kept in here is not for the eyes of one so young."

Again I pointed to the cupboard. "Little girl," I muttered.

Aunt Nellie listened with her ear to the cupboard door. She tutted. She placed her hand in her pocket and produced the key that would open the door. Her stout figure impeded my view of what lay inside and it was closed again before I was able to re-angle my position. She turned round, the transistor radio that normally lived in the kitchen, was held firmly in her hand.

"You silly boy, it's only the radio, I must have left it on."

She switched it off and left the room in a huff. How was I to know it was just a radio play? I never understood then why she'd put the radio in the cupboard and I'm none the wiser now.

After all those years I thought I would at last be able to see inside the cupboard. But as always it was locked. Those wondrous mysteries in Aunt Nellie's Cupboard have gone with her to her grave.

Autumn's Beck (*)

Gilbert was captivated by the sight of dust particles caught in a shaft of light coming from a small window high up in the church hall. He was greeted by a reassuring musty smell that one finds in old books and private letters. There was a consistent flow of prospectors all nosing amongst the bric-a-brac eager to sniff out a bargain.

You could almost cut the hypocrisy with a knife. Gilbert thought these pompous fools wouldn't know art if it jumped out and bit them. Still, the vicar is always glad to see them. He probably takes more money at these auctions than he does in a month of Sunday Services.

The familiarity of a painting in one corner attracted Gilbert's attention. His eyes confirmed his suspicion; it was his very own Autumn's Beck, now allocated the legend Lot 161.

As he peered at the painting he could feel the cool crisp air tight on his face. Blowing his hands in a vain attempt to keep the circulation going he wondered how long he could eke out the hot coffee in his flask. It was a bit early in the morning for a young student to be out on the riverbank with his paints and brushes, but he was destined to win the college art competition at his first attempt.

From his vantage point he could see as far as the flint bridge. He half expected to see Farmer

Chisholm leading his flock of sheep. He'd be lucky to see a fisherman but at least he wouldn't be pestered by courting couples or dogs and masters out for their evening walk.

This painting was to be no cheap souvenir for the holiday makers. The last of those invaders had long since staggered back to their coaches leaving the jetty sadly alone without its boats. No one would remain to watch dead leaves floating aimlessly down stream.

Many birds were preparing to migrate; they'd soon fly over the country hills, not to return until the following spring. The robin would stay: he could survive the hardest of winters and seemed oblivious to my presence.

That's all history, along with the minutes of a thousand committee meetings which decided to turn the area into a featureless reservoir. The robin has moved out and the yuppies have moved in. With their gaudy yacht and wind surfing boards they'd never care. Autumn's Beck is the only reminder of what has long since been forgotten.

An absurdity of a hundred times more than the original prize money was reserved for Lot 161. Should an artist suffer the indignity of paying so much for what cost him so little? Was it not his by right? Should he allow another bidder to have something that mattered so much but meant so little?

The vicar stood smiling at the back of the hall, much needed cash had been pledged. The hammer came down for Lot 161. Autumn's Beck was now where it belonged.

A Winter's Tale? - She's Mad, She Is! (*)

Terry was under pressure. His parents had spent a lot of money towards his keep at University. He didn't want to let them down but his last two assignments weren't up to scratch. Initially his Tutor was full of praise, even reading his work to the class, but just lately, Terry began to wonder if he'd lost his touch.

He'd over slept this morning and had missed an important lecture. The phone rang, it was his friend, Mark Bailey.

"Hello Terry. Where were you? We've got to write a story about a winter's tale. It's got to be in by end of the week."

"A winter's tale? She's mad, she is! I need to feel the cold blast of snow and ice, wind and rain, I can't do that when it's ninety degrees. One of the hottest days on record and she wants me to write about winter!"

He sweated over it for a bit and then resolved to read some meteorological articles. This would entail a trip to the Municipal Library, though he half hoped to see Amanda, the pretty library assistant. He would have to borrow his parent's car.

It was so hot in the car it was like a greenhouse. Terry wound down the windows gasping for air but it made little difference. The steering wheel was so hot he needed the coolness of sun cream, rubbed into his hands, before he could grip it. He drove off, squinting through his sun glasses, his clothes drenched in sweat.

Terry was horrified to see the temperature gauge on red. His hot temper soon boiled over when he lifted the bonnet. The radiator was gushing water and forming Lake Ontario beneath the engine.

The breakdown service whined a feeble apology. There was nothing for it he'd have to take the bus into town.

Thirty minutes later and Terry was still waiting. You've heard the old saying about two buses coming along at once? Not two, but four buses came. Four private companies all competing for the same service at the same time. Were they prepared to stagger their time schedules in the interests of the public? No chance!

"The wonders of privatisation at its best," Terry mused.

He went to board the first bus in the queue. An old man grabbed his arm.

"Don't get on that one unless you've got a weekly pass. If you're only going one way get on the third bus. Otherwise buy a return on the fourth bus, if you intend travelling back before peak hours, or the second one if you aren't."

Terry took the old man's advice and boarded the fourth one. What are the odds on someone's car breaking down and then the same thing happening to the bus? It happened to Terry. A mile from his destination and there he was: staggering up the hill towards the library. It was either that or wait another half hour for the relief bus.

Like a man who'd walked for days in a desert, Terry staggered through the library's doorway gasping for water. Where was the pretty library assistant? She was nowhere to be seen. He got no sympathy from the buxom lady that stood before him.

"Can I help you?" she barked.

He retreated to the shop next door and bought a can of drink before returning to the library. Wondering off to the Reference Section he suddenly espied Amanda, filing some books on the shelves. Spurred on by this lucky break he approached her boldly.

"Hi, Amanda, I didn't think you were working today?"

"It's my turn in the Reference Section today. Didn't I see you here last Tuesday?'

"No I had two vital lectures last Tuesday. I was on Campus all day."

"I thought you was from the University. Do you know Mark Bailey?'

Terry's heart sank: "Oh yes, he's going out with Jenny Shepherd?"

The conversation came to an abrupt halt. Amanda turned and left without any explanation.

Terry looked at the ground but it refused to open up and swallow him.

He wrote a tree load of information on how snow is formed and why temperatures change so much. But for all that, he didn't have a story. All those facts and figures, but no plot. There was nothing else for it but to get the bus home.

What are the chances of this bus breaking down? It wouldn't happen, says you. You're right. It didn't!

Glad to be home again he sat at his computer. He thought of winter. Once he'd a firm picture of heavily fallen snow, in his mind, he began to type.

"Terry put on his heavy coat, bobble hat and Wellington boots before stepping outside onto the freshly fallen snow..."

The phone rang. It was Mark.

"Hi Terry, where have you been? I've been ringing you for hours!"

"I've been to the library in town."

"What for?"

"To get some information for that assignment."

"What assignment?"

"That Winter's Tale one."

There was a muffled sound of laughter. Terry had yet again fallen for one of Mark's practical jokes.

"Do you fancy a pint tonight, Mark?'

"No I can't tonight. I'm seeing that Amanda from the library. Some guys get all the luck, don't they, Terry?"

Terry felt a guilty tingle of triumph. He remembered what he'd said to Amanda earlier. Mark had played one practical joke too many.

Blackbird, Bye Bye

BB lay injured in muddy soil, caught in a nightmare of senseless violence. Anarchy ruled. Battles raged for days. Homes were damaged. Blood was spilt.

Racism was out of control. The population had grown too large - there were too many mouths to feed and not enough food. Many were homeless and without land to build homes. Every race blamed one other. In truth, they were all to blame regardless of their colour of skin or nationality. They were warned it would happen, but they chose to ignore it. Now it was too late.

BB knew nothing about politics. She was just an innocent young blackbird recently flown from her mother's nest. She'd been used to her mother providing food whenever she needed it.

"BB, it's time you made your own way in the World. Go fly my precious BB, discover what life has to offer. One day, I hope, you'll come visit me with grandchildren."

And so BB went. But now she lay facing death. She remembered something else her mother had said.

"BB, when all may seem lost, never give up. Never give up until your dying breath."

BB struggled to break free, from the thick mud, but her wings were damaged. She needed strength, but it had forsaken her.

Her rescue was as unlikely as it was dramatic. A parrot swooped down and lifted BB to safety. Just a few seconds later, BB would have been trampled to death by an angry mob.

BB was very weak for several days afterwards but the parrot managed to nurse her back to health. The parrot's bright colours had fascinated BB. She'd never seen a parrot before.

"My name's Perch. I'm a Blue Frontal Amazon Parrot, captured from my homeland and brought here. I've spent the last few years of my life in a cage, but I escaped and I'm going to fly home to freedom."

"Can anyone go to Freedom? Is it a nice home? Why aren't you black like me? My mother's black and so are my brothers and sisters. You've got lots of colours. Green, yellow, blue, red. You're very handsome."

Perch chirped. He explained that where he came from all the birds looked like him. BB was very excited.

"Will you take me with you, Perch? I would love to go with you."

"Provided you can keep up with me I will be glad to take you. But are you sure about this, BB? What would your mother think?"

"Mother would approve, I know she would. She says I should always follow my instincts and they tell me to go with you."

Perch nodded: "Very well, we'll fly tomorrow, as soon as dawn breaks."

They flew south. Away from the rioting and fighting below them. BB had turned her back on the greed and stupidity that had consumed her world. Fighting and killing made no sense to her but her new world would give her fresh hope.

She'd a long flight ahead of her but she was prepared for it. Perch had warned her about the thunder and lightning they were likely to encounter. There'd be gale force winds to contend with as well as heavy rain. Perch was there to help her. He sheltered her from all the weathers Mother Nature had to offer.

Eventually the storms subsided and they'd made it to Perch's homeland. The sun was hot but the trees in the forest shaded them from it. BB was the happiest blackbird on Earth - she'd everything she could wish for. A lovely new home and a wonderful friend in Perch.

Many more parrots made their home there but her peace was soon threatened. BB was soon to learn that some of them weren't as friendly as Perch.

"Go back to where you came from. Your black skin's not welcomed around here."

They spat and bit BB. They'd hurt her and she was very frightened. Why was she being treated this way? What was wrong with her black skin? She was flesh and blood just like them.

"You don't belong here. Blackbird, bye, bye."

Perch soon came to her rescue. He flapped his wings and screeched loudly forcing these parrots to retreat.

"You won't always have your precious friend here to help you. Then we'll finish you off. You Black Bitch!"

This made Perch very angry. He screeched and pecked at the cowardly parrots until they all fled.

Over the coming months Perch was to keep a close eye on BB to make sure that nothing attacked her. She started to grow bigger and stronger. As the seasons progressed the parrots began to accept her and within a year the racial abuse had ceased. Everyone had grown to love BB.

But soon more animals reached the forest. Birds flew in from the sky, whilst reptiles and some mammals emerged from the sea. Others came overland.

Perch lay badly injured in muddy soil, caught in a nightmare of senseless violence. Anarchy ruled. Battles raged for days. Homes were damaged. Blood was spilt.

Racism was out of control. The population had grown too large - there were too many mouths to feed and not enough food. Many were homeless and without land to build homes. Every race blamed one other. In truth, they were all to blame regardless of their colour of skin or nationality. They were warned it would happen, but they chose to ignore it. Now it was too late.

Perch's rescue was as unlikely as it was dramatic. BB swooped down and lifted him to safety. Just a few seconds later, Perch would have been trampled to death by an angry mob.

BB managed to nurse him back to health. They flew further south, turning their backs on the rioting and fighting. They would find a new world. But this time they'd see to it that greed and stupidity were words to be forgotten.

Bob's Father And The Spy

Driving steadily along the road one misty winter's night, disapproving headlights shone brightly in my rear view mirror. If the driver behind had got any closer he would have surely touched my bumper. Accelerating to the speed limit would not pacify and the headlights behind seemed to glow angrier when I dared to slow down.

Bob MacDonald was my passenger that night as was on many occasions. Old Bob had long since given up driving and I was happy to give him a lift whenever I could. Bob could see that I was getting irritated by the car behind but told me not to be intimidated by it.

"Just ignore him," he said. "Now when I was a wee boy."

That was his introduction to his story. Bob had a hundred and one stories to tell but this was his favourite and I was about to hear it for the hundredth time. Whether this story is entirely true or not I don't know, or if indeed any of his tales are, I would wager though Bob was at least prone to exaggeration.

Bob was brought up in the Shetland Islands during the Second World War and his father served as a pilot in the RAF. During the war years Bob never got to see much of his father but on one fateful night Bob unwittingly embarked on a dangerous mission with his Dad.

Bob's best friend in Shetland was a lad in his class called Jimmy Leask. Now at this point Bob would witter on, going into great detail about his friendship with Jimmy but his friend played little part in this story. So I will just say they were out playing one evening when they both realised they wouldn't make it home before dark. Unless, of course, they cut across Farmer Reid's field which had a fierce bull in it which they called Bully.

To cut another long story short Bob's mother had a terrifying temper and Bob decided he would risk confrontation with Bully rather than face his Mum's chastisement. In any case, they could outwit a bull couldn't they?

So they started to creep across the field and tried to keep as quiet as possible. As they crept they became aware of a plane landing at the bottom end of the field. This wasn't unusual. Planes on the island were part and parcel of every day life and Farmer Reid was agreeable for the RAF to use his field. Shetland is a wild place which has long severe winters and its summers are scarcely luke warm. Yet despite this the long days during the summer months and the absence of trees made it ideal for small planes to land.

Needless to say as they began crossing the field Bully started charging towards them. Jimmy was quickly out of the field to safety but Bob instinctively ran towards the plane which by now had landed and the pilot had vacated the cockpit. With Bully on his heals Bob scrambled onto the plane and dived behind the pilot's seat. Peering out the window from time to time Bob could see Bully wasn't giving up and was waiting patiently for Bob to come out. There was nothing else for it but for Bob to wait until the pilot returned and perhaps he could scare off Bully.

Time went by and Bob had fallen asleep but eventually he was woken to the sound of the plane's engine. To his horror he realised the plane had taken off. He was in for it now. He was in serious trouble. Confined to his bedroom for at least a month and the hiding of his life no doubt. The pilot wasn't going to be too pleased either.

The pilot was indeed shocked to find a young boy in the back and even more so to discover it was his son. What was Bob's father to do with him? He couldn't turn back to Shetland. He was on a very important mission and time was at the essence but he had his son on board.

"The Germans won't get us, Dad".

"It's not the Germans I'm worried about, son. Your mother will crucify me. The air will turn blue, lad."

Bob didn't know what his father meant. How can air turn blue? He didn't question his father but air is colourless, isn't it? At least his Science teacher

Mr Campbell said so and he was always right about these things.

Bob learned from his father they were heading to Norway to rescue a British spy and return him safely to Shetland. Bob's father wouldn't reveal the name of the spy and Bob never did learn his identity. So Bob, being a practical and simplistic man, always referred to him as Spy.

Spy had secret papers on him for which Churchill was very keen to get his hands on and his agent's capture had to be avoided at all costs. Spy was being helped by the Norwegian Resistance Movement who gave him food and shelter. The Germans were out in numbers searching for him but heavy snow and freezing conditions were hindering their search. On the other hand the wintery weather would also make it more difficult for Spy to escape the country.

The Resistance had seen to it information was leaked to the Germans Spy would attempt to cross the border into neutral Sweden. This would happen, the Germans were told, on the last day of April 1943. Whilst they lay in wait, keeping watch on all entries to Sweden, some twenty miles from the border Bob's father was to land his plane and pick up his passenger. The Resistance and other volunteers had worked tirelessly to clear the snow from a field to enable the plane to land.

The risks were high. Bob's father had to hope he would avoid confrontation with German planes and somehow land in Norway unnoticed. It would be dark when he landed and it was important the makeshift runway would be sufficiently lit.

On the flight over Bob learned a few things about his father he never knew before and you could say they bonded for the first time. Bob was surprised to learn there was a time when Glasgow Rangers were very interested in signing his father but a leg injury had ended that dream. Bob was in awe. Glasgow Rangers! Wow!

His father was also a keen gardener, which Bob was aware of, but he never knew the extent of it until then. Hs father had built a large greenhouse in their family garden, which was often heated to enable all sorts of fruit and veg to grow which wouldn't have survived the Shetland climate otherwise. Suddenly a new world had opened up to Bob. He was fascinated to hear about seedlings, fertilisers and especially compost. The thought of all those worms and creepy crawlies doing their stuff was somehow very exciting to a young boy. He wanted his father to teach him all he knew about gardening when they got back, if they got back, but right now there were other matters pressing.

The driver behind me finally decided to over take me much to my relief. As the car passed, Bob wound down his window with his fist punching the air, he shouted abuse at the passing driver. There was no point in this, the driver would have never understood Bob's broad Scottish accent even if he could have heard him. With a cold blast of wind coming through the open window I pleaded with Bob to close it immediately. Fortunately he did so and returned to his story; this wasn't perhaps so fortunate for me but it was better than freezing to death.

The time had come. Luckily the weather conditions were favourable and the clear skies helped Bob's father to see his makeshift runway. Bob was told to lie down on the floor and on no circumstances was he to look out of the window. For once Bob did as he was told and later admitted he was very scared.

The plane landed and was brought to a halt as quickly as Bob's father was able. Out from nowhere came Spy running towards the plane but bullets flew passed narrowly missing him. It seems, by chance, a German patrol had spotted what was happening and had opened fire. Members of the Resistance fired back and no sooner had Spy boarded the plane when it was turning round and heading back up the runway. As Bob lay low he shivered in fright, a number bullets hit the plane and he could feel the vibration around him. The noise was deafening. At any moment he thought a bullet would hit the fuel tank and the plane would burst into flames. Somehow no serious damage was caused and soon they were back in the air. Below the German patrol had been taken care of and the runway lights were extinguished.

Although back in flight their troubles weren't over yet. Several German fighter planes had spotted them and were heading in their direction. Bob's father had the advantage of a very fast aircraft and speed would be his best defence. His pursuers were not gaining ground but from the other direction more German planes were approaching. Skillfully he turned the plane ninety degrees and flew in and out of a series of clouds which served to confuse the enemy. He had successfully avoided the oncoming planes but now he had half a dozen of them in pursuit. Then several more aircraft were approaching and just when it all seemed lost, miraculously a large number of British fighter planes arrived which gave Bob's father the chance to slip away.

Eventually they made it back safely to Shetland and Spy was transported to mainland Scotland before returning to London and to a grateful Churchill. Whitehall praised Bob's father for his actions but he wasn't so popular with his wife. Bob learned that day what his father meant by "the air will turn blue."

As I pulled outside Bob's house it was time for him to finish up his story. Usually at this point Bob would deviate from his tale and tell me about his career as a gardener and this time would be no exception. After the war and after he had left school, Bob went to college and gained his necessary qualifications to become a professional gardener. He worked in a number of gardens on the mainland before moving to the South of England and taking up the position of Head Gardener in a privately owned estate. This time though, I was thankful for small mercies, Bob had refrained from telling me one of his garden stories of which there a many.

Returning to his favourite story and with the engine still running he told me his mother had wept that day as she cradled him in her arms. She thought she would never see him again. Bob got out of my car but then popped his head in the doorway. Bob then chuckled like he always did.

"Then Mother gave me a bloody good hiding."

Boxed In **

We all live in some kind of a box; so you want me to take the lid off yours!

You're an ambitious man in a very competitive world. Meeting targets is very important to you. The constant pursuit of perfection gives you less and less margin for error. I can understand why you have doubts about your own ability.

So what would happen if you became the Sales Director? What would your goal be then? I wonder if you've really thought about that.

On that particular day, you were on your way to work when some roadworks forced you to take an unfamiliar route. The traffic was reduced to a crawl, which would be frustrating for anyone, but for you it was a nightmare. On a day you needed to be at your best you were now late for a meeting.

Gazing out of the car your eyes rested on some cardboard boxes almost hidden in a shop doorway. Slowly, you realised that there was someone lying in the boxes, in fact, there were several people huddled together trying to keep warm.

Faced with this poverty you felt bewildered and uncomfortable; a wave of revulsion came over you. Had the other drivers seen what you'd seen or couldn't they bring themselves to look either?

It was easy for you to dismiss it from the comfort of your company car. But what if you didn't meet your targets or if a better man came along and took your place?

That is why you were unable to help those people. You'd come face to face with your worst fears as you realised you would be nothing without the trappings of your success. Unable to get out of the car - unable to get out of the rat race.

The Challenge

If I'd ever needed my competitive spirit it was then. In tennis, I'm known for chasing after every shot and in my younger days I could be seen sprinting all over the football pitch. But this time I wasn't pursuing - I was being pursued.

Although crabs live in the sea I was chased in the hot desert by a giant crab about forty foot high. My heartbeat was like a drum roll and sweat ran freely down my face. Just about keeping my feet, I looked over my shoulder to see this monster gaining ground on me by the second. I had a vision of being cooked alive and then eaten for its dinner. Poetic justice for its much smaller relative, perhaps, but why pick on a vegetarian like me?

I'd no time to reason why a Victorian house should be standing in the middle of the desert, but with nowhere else to go I hid inside. Within seconds the crab had reached the house and its shell covered the roof. Its pincers pierced through the bricks and came within a foot of me. Dust fell from the ceiling, the walls crumbled, broken glass was everywhere.

Knees knocking, body shaking with fear, my legs somehow got me across the room. Without hesitation I leapt into the dumb waiter, only to find myself falling at high speed down the shaft. Incredibly my fall was broken by soft cushions.

Still frightened, I got to my feet and ran blindly down a tunnel. I followed a light which led to some steep steps. Climbing them, I stepped into a garden.

When I stopped to catch my breath, I looked back and the crab had virtually crushed the house. I heard a buzzing noise which became louder as it drew nearer. I was horrified to see a swarm of bees heading towards me and not in the mood to share their honey with me.

Fortunately there were no piranha fish or hungry alligators when I plunged into the river which was conveniently situated at the bottom of the garden. Swimming below the surface to escape the bees deadly sting, I prayed that they wouldn't realise I couldn't stay under water for long.

I struggled to break free as a whirlpool sucked me towards the bottom. Down and down I plummeted, my life flashing before me, the water was becoming black and dirty. I hit the bottom and became trapped in a jet of water that shot me to the surface and spat me out like a piece of poisonous fruit.

I passed out and awoke in a haystack. All was quiet and still. Although scared, I took comfort in the knowledge nothing would surprise me any more. I should have known better to be complacent after all that had happened to me.

Lightning flashed across the sky and I could hear the thunder rumbling. The wind was blowing so fiercely I was hardly able to stand up. Dodging pieces of timber and hay that flew from all directions, I ran and ran but there was no running from a hurricane. I was lifted off the ground and thrown about a hundred yards.

Wind whistling in my ears, dust blowing in my eyes, sheer determination got me up again and instinctively I ran southwards. Again I was thrown but miraculously I landed in a sheltered spot. Making the most of my good fortune I made my way down a zigzag pathway and discovered it led to a cave. Gratefully I crawled inside.

It was dark, damp and cold. Stalactite were all around. I'd no idea where the cave would lead but it was preferable to the mighty hurricane. Tired and weary I rested for a while. I thought about my family and friends but mostly the one I loved. I wondered if I'd ever see her again and if this nightmare would ever cease.

I knew the lack of activity wouldn't last long and a score of angry bats confirmed my fears. They attacked me relentlessly and every time I tried to stand up they knocked me down again. I rolled along the ground. Then, clutching hold of a stake, I set it alight. Swinging the torch in a circular motion I stood up. The cowardly bats fled as my hysterical laughter echoed against the walls.

Reaching the end of the cave led me to an exit and I was relieved to be out in the open air once more. I reflected on how I'd behaved in there and realised how close to madness I'd become.

I felt as if my ordeal was finally over. I whistled and skipped with a spring in my step as I made my way across the plain. But then I got this feeling I wasn't alone. Unfortunately, I was horribly right.

Advancing from the east on horseback and on the war-path was a Red Indian Tribe. Charging, bugle blowing, flag flying, the United States Cavalry galloped from the west. There I was, smack bang in the middle and the end was in sight. I was almost past the post and they'd thrown this at me. I fled southwards.

Arrows and bullets flew over my head as the finishing line drew nearer. I puffed out my cheeks, clenched my fists and I crossed the line like an Olympic Champion. Mentally exhausted, the assistant removed my Virtual Reality headset. The machine said I'd scored well and I'd qualified for the next round. I declined, preferring to keep my sanity. I left the amusement park.

At home I sat down and watched one of those tame James Bond films which were so popular in the last century. They've recorded it onto DDDMCCD now but nothing can be done with a primitive film recording.

I pondered on what I'd experienced that day. Perhaps I could have a go at trying to beat the current Wimbledon Champion? If not, I could score the winning penalty in the 2038 World Cup Final!

Christmas Spirit

The wind blew at gale force speed, shaking the trees and almost uplifting their roots. The rain, though, had stopped and the mild temperature for the time of year could hardly be considered seasonal. The once traditional setting of pure white snow, that would cover the ground like a blanket, was restricted now to picture postcards. Parents no longer watched from their windows as their children built snowmen or threw snowballs at one another. Children have much more sophisticated pastimes now and expensive computer games are at the top of many a child's list. Similarly, the tradition of families spending Christmas at home is beginning to change. Some families even spend an extended holiday abroad in a warmer climate. Others settle for a few days away in some scenic hotel and many will just simply trade-in their home cooking in exchange for an al la carte menu.

The hotel guests in a pretty Cotswold's Village had broken with tradition and didn't seem to mind that the weather wasn't picturesque. In fact, for those whom had travelled, the absence of snow was welcomed. Inside the dinning room everyone was ready to tuck into some Christmas spirit and some wore silly hats as they all sat at tables of various covers and colours. There were parties of ten or more and mums and dads with their children. There were groups of four as well as couples young and old. Then there was a table laid just for one.

The inconspicuous old man sat at this table opposite his conspicuous missing partner. Where was this person? Had he always been on his own or was this something new he'd have to get used to? Where did this man come from - sitting amongst fifty or more guests and yet quite alone? These questions begged an answer if only they'd been asked. What exciting stories a man of his experience may have had to tell of Christmases that had come and gone. Bravely he joined in the Christmas jollities as best he could, but pulling his own cracker would cause somewhat of a problem. The waiter dutifully obliged and exchanged a few words of conversation with the old man.

Any feelings of self pity would surely of evaporated as he stared out the window and across the street to the small cottage that stood all alone. Its door bell had lost its chime and its knocker was no longer at home. Slates had fallen from its roof, leaving the wind to whistle in the loft, disturbing the nests of more than one family. Whilst paint had but all flaked off the windows which had left the seals to gradually rot.

An old lady occupied the cottage and was in her kitchen preparing her Christmas lunch. It was painfully clear that she was all alone and there would be no traditional Christmas fayre for her - just a few tins of food would have to do.

Her husband's estate would keep her above the bread line but it couldn't stretch to Christmas dinner at the hotel opposite. She couldn't be doing with meals on wheels despite her failing eyesight and crippled hands. Even opening something as simple as a tin caused her difficulty, let alone preparing a wholesome meal.

She sat down at her old wooden dining table complimented by her old wooden chair and she began eating her soup. She'd a few slices of bread left but had shared some of this with the robin whom had sung with expectancy outside her kitchen window.

She had nothing to complain about she thought as her heart went out to the tramp whom had just walked by her window. In need of a bath and some clean clothes, the soles of his shoes had worn through to the bottoms of his holly socks. His rags offered little protection against the wind and he staggered down the hotel's alley for shelter.

He scavenged amongst the dustbins until he found a few dog ends but there'd be no dinner for him that day. From one of his pockets he produced some cigarette papers and he carefully tipped the tobacco from the dog ends into them. From another pocket he pulled out a box of matches and striking one of them, he lit his rolled cigarette. He inhaled vigorously and blew out a few puffs of smoke before the tobacco had burnt out. He continued with this until he'd smoked the remaining dog end and he then settled down contented with his bottle of coke.

He could see into the dinning room and he felt sorry for the old man sitting on his own by the window. The tramp counted his blessings, he'd sensed that the old man would be alone that night and for the rest of the festive season. Although the tramp was on his own at that moment, sitting amongst the hotel dustbins, that night he and Scotty would have a party back at the squat. Just the two of them mind. Although it was cold and damp, they would light a fire to keep the chilled air at bay. As their Christmas treat, the bottle of whisky they'd managed to pilfer would lift their spirits and warm their souls.

The old lady sat down by the gas fire and drank her mug of tea. The tramp guzzled his bottle of coke and licked his lips in anticipation. The old man was now staring aimlessly out of the window as he sipped his glass of brandy. Christmas spirit was in full flow.

The Columbus Story (Fictional Article)

Mention the name Christopher Columbus and most people will think of the man who discovered America. Actually he wasn't the first. Apart from the indigenous people who already lived there, Leif Ericson had arrived some five hundred years before in a failed attempt to coach Football Soccer to the natives. Leif Ericson's descendant Sven Goram Ericson, who was the voice for the Muppet Show's Swedish Chef, also failed in his attempt to win trophies for England.

The question is: would Columbus have wanted to be remembered for discovering America? Has the World benefited or would things have been better if it had been left to the Apache Tribe to rule America. It is worth acknowledging it Columbus's Great Great Great Great Great Grandson, Kris Columbus, who formed Columbia Records and the Shadows had a number one hit with their tribute to the Apache in 1960. Columbia Records was to expand over the years and one spin off label was named after Columbus's mother Susanna Fontanarossa and was called The Fontana Label. Furthermore the son of Kris Columbus, also Christopher Columbus, became a filmmaker.

A national survey was conduced to establish if English people were for or against America as we know it. Some 60% of those surveyed cited as irritating the misspelling of words such as Color instead of Colour. More than 75% hated words which were pronounced incorrectly. Schedule pronounced skedule was at the top of the list with almost 50% of the 75% suggesting such an act warranted ten years hard labour. 77% disliked words like sidewalk and 80% despised the phrase "check this out". An overwhelming 95% couldn't abide those "God Damn dreadful America Cop shows". Ironically one of the better Cop programmes was Colombo (Latin name for Columbus) which was based on a true American Detective of the same name. Of those in favour of the USA, a staggering 99% said life would be unimaginable if America hadn't have given us the Marx Brothers.

It is believed Columbus was born around 1451 and any suggestions he was born in the morning have been dismissed. It is thought he was born between August and October which made it an incredibly long and frustrating labour particularly as his mother had always been Tory. His father, Domenico Colombo, got so impatient with waiting to wet the baby's head he wet himself instead.

Columbus received some education although he claimed to have gone to sea when he was ten. What he went to see is not clear but he was far more ambitious than his father and wasn't content with helping him run a cheese stand although this was the inspiration for a famous television sketch. It is believed in 1470 Columbus was on a ship on course to conquer the Kingdom Of Naples whilst his father, in keeping with his son's connections with the sea, took over a Bass tavern. Unfortunately he was forced to give it up due to ill health brought on by the draughts from the cellar. In 1473 Columbus began an apprenticeship as a business agent for the Genoa family. It was centuries later before the Genoas became wealthy when the handsome David Genoa signed for Newcastle and later finished his career with Spurs.

In 1476 Columbus took part in an armed convoy sent by the Genoas to carry a valuable cargo to northern Europe. He docked in Bristol and witnessed City and Rovers battle it out one Saturday afternoon. He then sailed across the Irish Sea to Galway but had to return to Bristol when he realised he'd left his boat behind. When he eventually arrived in Galway he was disappointed to find James wasn't at home and so he headed to Iceland for some frozen supplies. In 1479 Columbus joined his brother Bartolomeo for some sport in Lisbon. He later married Filipa Moniz Perestrello, daughter of the Porto Santo governor, the Portuguese nobleman of Genoese origin Bartolomeu Perestrello. It was much relief to her to be now known as simply Mrs Columbus.

With the fall of Constantinople to the Turks in 1453, the once safe passage to China and India had become more difficult. Captain Fry of the Turkish Fleet was largely credited with this capture much to the delight of the Turkish people. So happy were they even to this day it is commemorated in Turkey as "Fry's Turkish Delight Day". Due to the problem of unsafe passage Columbus and his brothers had constructed a plan in 1480 to travel to the Indies and beyond by sailing directly west across the Atlantic Ocean. It is commonly believed Columbus had difficulty gaining support for his plan because the Europeans believed the World was flat. In fact even primitive maritime navigation relied on the stars and the curvature of the spherical Earth. Moreover Ancient Greek Science had supported this view since the 4th Century although they were reluctant to reveal the circumference of the Earth with other scientists. They would only "Gift" this information as they put it if they received something in exchange. That something usually involved valuable merchandise and even then they didn't always pass on the correct mathematical calculations. In most cases their "Gift" was worthless; hence the saying "Beware of Greeks bearing gifts".

It was only the uneducated man who thought that the World was flat mainly because the rulers of Europe encouraged them to believe this. Even in those days there were environmental concerns and these had become a hot potato ever since Sir Walter Raleigh, inventor of the bicycle, had discovered the vegetable. To ensure energy was conserved, it was thought if people believed the World was flat it would discourage them travelling for fear of going over the edge. Columbus didn't believe that the World was flat but neither did he share the educated view of a spherical one. He was convinced the World was a triangle and tried to persuade the European rulers this theory was the correct one. Everyone of course thought he was barking mad and laughed at his triangle theory but Columbus stuck to his guns. He had used strong glue and it took several men to have enough strength to unstick him from his weapons.

Columbus had been strongly influenced by Baricus Manicolo a wandering minstrel who toured the streets of Europe singing about the Bermuda Triangle. Columbus's theorised the Earth was much smaller than what was widely believed and was convinced Asia was only a few thousand miles to the west of Europe. His maths were inaccurate even though he'd used a calculator. His school teacher had written "see me" on his homework on many occasions but Maths just wasn't his best subject. He hadn't taken into account the ships available in those days couldn't carry enough food and fresh water and there were no fast food outlets such as Little Chef to break up the journey. How lucky they were in those days. His poor eye sight didn't help matters either and nor did his low quality spectacles. Fellow seaman were later to declare: "He should have gone to Specsavers."

Columbus's chances of finding a backer for his adventure were very slim given his triangle World theory and his suspect mathematical calculations. His chances were so poor it seemed more likely England would win a penalty shoot out. Well, okay, his chances weren't that slim but the odds were against him. In 1485 he presented his plans to King John of Portugal and proposed the King equip three sturdy ships and allow Columbus one year to search for a western route to Orient. Even though King John suggested a trip to neighbouring West Ham would be more desirable given their superior status, he still put forward Columbus's proposal. King John's experts considered the proposal but they rejected it citing the lack of Arsenal as one good reason.

In 1488 Columbus tried again and again King John invited him to an audience. Columbus was a little wary of this and he wanted to know with whom the audience would be with. He'd been pleased with an audience with Bilious Connilous, a court jester, who told amusing stories with colourful language. Bilious was famous for his thick accent, long hair and bushy beard which was to be his trade mark for most of his career. In any event the arrival of Bartholomeu Dias, Portugal's native son, from a successful trip to Africa meant Portugal were no longer interested in a western route to the East.

At one point Henry VII of England showed some interest in Columbus's proposal. A fortune teller had looked into Henry's crystal ball and predicted Henry's son, Henry VIII, would have six wives and the thought of having so many daughter-in-laws would drive him mad. He reasoned perhaps Columbus could take these women on a long voyage before his son could become acquainted. This idea was to come to nothing for Henry VII died and his son became King.

Columbus then laid his plans at the feet of Ferdinand and Isabella the monarchs of Spain. Isabella picked the plans up off the floor and referred this to a committee but, like Portugal, they suggested Columbus had judged the distance to Asia too short. They advised Ferdinand and Isabella to pass on the proposed venture but to keep Columbus from going elsewhere they gave him a large annuity. In 1489 they furnished him with a letter and whilst Columbus would rather have had tables and chairs for furniture; the letter ordered all Spanish cities and towns to provide him with free food and lodging.

After continually lobbying the Spanish Court for two years Columbus finally succeeded in 1492. Ferdinand and Isabella had just conquered Granada and had set their sights on ATV. Isabella had turned Columbus down on the advice of her confessor but

Ferdinand intervened just as Columbus was leaving in despair. He could have left in a horse and carriage but decided on despair. Ferguson, Ferdinand's manager, had suggested to him that he should take a chance on Columbus as this would be good publicity for the monarchs. Columbus had already lined up private Italian investors and the monarchs left it to Captain Kirk to shift funds among various royal accounts for the enterprise. Columbus was to be made "Admiral Of The Seas" and would receive a portion of all profits but secretly nobody expected him to return.

On the night of 3rd August, 1492, Columbus departed with three ships; one larger Carrack, Santa Maria, captained by Paul. The other were two smaller caravels, Pinta and Santa Clara. To have two ships with the name Santa was a surprise for nobody realised Columbus believed in Father Christmas. The ships were the property of Juan del la Cosa and the Pinzon brothers, a well known musical hall act, for whom the monarchs had forced a financial contribution. Columbus sailed to the Canary Islands with a parrot on his shoulder and there he restocked for provisions and made repairs before departing on a five week voyage across the ocean.

Land was sighted at 2 a.m. on 12th October, 1492, which is know today as The Bahamas and there he encountered friendly people and communicated with them with sign language. It hadn't occurred to him to bring his Bahamas phrase book with him mainly because one was yet to be written. Before returning to Spain Columbus went to Cuba where he was greeted by the Gibson natives and they entertained him by singing "Cuba" the then National Anthem and other songs such as "Oh What A Life." Following his musical entertainment he smoked cigars whilst The Cuban Players performed Hamlet.

More voyages were to follow before Columbus would eventually land in America. On his second voyage Columbus left Spain on 24 September, 1493 with 17 ships and about 1,200 men. It was on 13 October he left the Canary Islands as he had done before but this time he took a left turning and followed a more southerly course. On 3 November Columbus sighted a rugged island which he named Dominica (Latin for Sunday) only it was actually Wednesday but nobody had the heart to tell him. Later that day he landed at Marie-Galante, which he named Santa Maria la Galante and by now many of his officers were beginning to believe he'd become obsessed with Father Christmas. After sailing past Los Santos, The Saints, he arrived at Santa Maria and then there was no doubt he was obsessed with Father Christmas. Further on his voyage he sighted the Virgin Islands, now governed by Branson, but at the time the islands were having a substantial problem with its birth-rate. On 22 November Columbus arrived at Hispaniola where he intended to visit Christmas Fort and by now his officers had become very worried about him. He reached Jamaica on 5 May and had lunch in the Jamaica Inn with his friend Daphne and Cardinal Bacardi. Columbus didn't much like the menu and made quite a fuss by complaining to the manager and witnesses to the incident said it was a right rum do.

On his third voyage Columbus left with six ships on 30 May, 1498 and was accompanied by Bartoome de Las Casa, who would later provide partial transcripts of Columbus's logs. Most of the logs of course ended up on the fire which were to keep Columbus warm during the cold winter nights. One of his officers was a much older man called Trinilous and for whom Columbus affectionately named "Trini." Columbus looked upon Trini as a fatherly figure and when Columbus discovered another new land he called this Trinidad in his honour.

When he returned to Hispaniola he found many of the Spanish settlers were unhappy with the new world. They claimed Columbus mislead them and some returned to Spain and lobbied against him in the Spanish Court. On his return Columbus was arrested and spent some time in prison but was later released to enable him to embark on a fourth voyage.

On his fourth voyage he was accompanied by his brother Bartoomeo and his 13 year old son Fernando. As they left Spain they were given a lively send off with crowds of people waiving at the docks and music playing as they set sail. Bartoome de Las Casa noted Columbus turned to his son and asked: "Can you hear the drums, Fernando?" Once at sea they were soon to run into a storm and, hoping to find shelter, they headed for Santa Domingo but were denied port and settled for sherry instead. Unfortunately the storm had caused considerable damage and it cost Columbus a lot of money to pay for the repairs. When Columbus was to later make a claim on the insurance he was furious when the insurance company refused to pay out. They said he wasn't covered for all risks and when taking the hefty excess into account there was no payment to make. Columbus realised he should have taken the trouble to obtain more quotes and he shouldn't have trusted the insurance broker Gone To Compare A Market Dot Com.

When Columbus finally landed in America the natives were waiting for him. This historical moment wasn't captured on camera but reliable records show the conversation went something like this.

Natives: Our ancestors warned us that you might return here one day.

Columbus: But I've never been here before in my life!

Natives: Don't get funny with me white man. White man came here five hundred years ago.

Columbus: That's not true, I am the first.

Natives: No you're not. White man Lief Ericson was first.

Columbus: Lief Ericson?

Natives: Taking a leaf out of his book are you?

Columbus: What?

Natives: You're wasting your time. We're not interested in your Football Soccer.

Columbus: Eh?

Natives: Or your Rugby.

Columbus: What's an English Town got to do with this?

Natives: We have our own game. American Football.

Columbus: American Football?

Natives: We don't want your Rounders either. We've got Baseball.

Columbus: Oh really?

Natives: Yes, we have our own World Series.

Columbus: I'm impressed. How many countries have joined your World Series?

Natives: Oh there's just us.

Despite the luke warm reception Columbus stayed long enough to colonise America which was to shape the USA as it is today. Of course it wasn't all plain sailing especially on dry land and the Hundred Years War which followed was marketed and encouraged to suit Hollywood. Columbus lived out the rest of his life a fairly wealthy man and his

"Triangle World" theory was never mentioned by him or anyone else again. There is a consensus of opinion which suggests Columbus never actually believed the World was anything but round but he'd put forward the triangle theory on the advise of his giddy spin doctors. Whatever the truth it had worked for Columbus for it got him noticed and one will never know whether he would have succeeded otherwise.

The Crunch *

No matter how hard I try I'm unable to break free. When the first bulldozer came through, it brought the apple tree down on top of me. The pain was indescribable but now I can't even feel my legs. I can hardly breathe. If I could muster a shout what good would it do now?

Crossley wouldn't hear but then he never listened. We went through all the right channels. We packed out the village hall - got them all to sign the petition. The local rag ran the story for weeks and we even had the support of our M.P.

But now it's come to the crunch, I'm the only one left. Everyone has scattered, like the pigeons from the clock tower when it strikes the hour. Like those scruffy kids scooting out of the cornfields every time Farmer comes by. Like they've always done whenever Crossley threatens to close the factory.

I knew that Crossley was a hard man but I never thought it would come to this. It's like being in a battlefield. Smoke and brick dust fills the air. The bulldozers must have demolished the back of the house. I watch helplessly as the slates cascade off the collapsing roof. The chimney pot crashed down missing me by inches.

So they call this progress. We've got enough roads already. I won't stand by and let them build another one through my village. This was my home and my life but now I'm all alone. There isn't time left now to feel betrayed.

Above the sound of the roaring bulldozers and shattering glass I fancy I hear the sound of police sirens. No it can't be. Amidst all this confusion I can hardly breathe. If I could muster a shout what good would it do now?

Donald MacKinnon's Boots **

It is now almost four minutes gone and Strathmuir are awarded a free kick thirty yards out from the goal line. Kirkthistle have four men in the wall as Donald MacKinnon shapes up to take the free kick. It's a swerving and viciously dipping shot and it's knocked the 'keeper into the back of the net. What a sensational goal, a hat-trick in the first four minutes...

It was nine o'clock on Friday evening. Roger MacKinnon awoke from his daydream and turned his attention back to tomorrow's vital match against the league leaders, The Nags Head. As he laid out his immaculately pressed shirt and shorts, he realised that they must win this one or they'll be doomed to relegation. Football is a serious business; pity his teammates didn't feel the same way. Boozing on a Friday night was no way to prepare for a match, he thought, as he finished his cocoa.

He gathered the rest of his gear; shin pads, tapes and liniment before applying dubbing to his football boots. His father the late, great Donald MacKinnon was always meticulous with his match preparation. He played inside left for Strathmuir and Scotland, collecting many honours including a Cup Final winner's medal. He holds the unique distinction of scoring a hat-trick in four minutes.

Donald's deeds were legendary. Sadly, Roger was too young to have witnessed his achievements. If only he could have been half the player his father was, he thought, as he zipped up his kit bag and went off to bed for an early night.

In the morning he was awoken by the sound of his demanding wife.

"Wake up, Roger, don't forget we've got to do the shopping."

"Do I have to? Can't you go by yourself? I've got to get ready for the match," complained Roger.

"For goodness sake, Roger, what's the matter with you? It's only a game. There are more important things in life, you know," his wife retorted.

She just didn't understand. She couldn't grasp the importance of such a vital fixture. The great Donald MacKinnon didn't have all this aggravation. Football always came first, that was understood. With a sigh Roger got dressed and dutifully went off to the supermarket with his wife.

There is a steady stream of people coming through the turnstiles; looks like it could be a capacity crowd today. A great buzz of anticipation sweeps through the tinned veg on the terraces. It could be a tactical battle today with Roger MacKinnon operating as an overlapping full back. Talk about taking your life into your own hands, as he weaves down the aisle with his shopping trolley outflanking the defence. Playing against the The

Nags Head's right back is nothing compared with taking on the old ladies in this supermarket. Mrs Black's the most formidable; clash with her at your peril.

Oooh! It's a nasty collision after a fifty-fifty ball between the trolley and the crisp packets..... it looks like the crisps have come off worst. The referee is going over to talk to Mrs. Black.... And, yes, she's been cautioned for deliberate obstruction. On comes the assistant with the 'magic sponge' to clean things up. Fortunately no-one's badly hurt. As the wife waves play on, they're back on their feet and Roger MacKinnon flies down the wing exchanging passes of soap powder, cakes and breakfast cereal. He prepares to take a corner by the vegetable stand but it's too late - it's half-time. As the crowd make its way to the refreshment stall; the players are trudging off to receive their half time talk.

Arriving home from the away fixture at the supermarket, Roger was greeted by his teammate Wally Burnes. Wally is the centre half, who has earned himself a reputation for his uncompromising tackles and is known, rather unkindly, in some circles as 'Third Degree Burnes'. Roger gathered his kit and picked up the size ten boots his father wore.

"I don't why you keep those old boots. Apart from being old fashioned they're far too big for you to play in," Wally pointed out.

"Nobody wears these boots," said Roger sharply, "only the great Donald MacKinnon could wear these boots...."

"Yeah, yeah, yeah, I know, I know," interrupted Wally, "he scored a hat-trick in four minutes wearing those boots. But what's the point of carting them round with you?"

"They're my mascot. A part of the MacKinnon heritage," replied Roger, "football's a tradition in our family."

"What tradition?" asked Wally. "Okay, so your dad was a professional footballer. No-one else in your family has been and you hardly fit that bill, do you Roger, playing inside left for the Rose and Crown."

Roger looked hurt by this remark. He would say no more. He'd always wanted to follow in his father's footsteps. If he could score the winner today, he'd like to think his father would have been proud of him.

They got into Roger's old estate car which had long since seen better days. It didn't start. Roger had desperately pumped the accelerator, but to no avail. There was nothing for it but call upon his son, Donald, who happened to be a very good car mechanic. Although he was named after the great man, the young Donald had no interest in football whatsoever. He had played at school because it was compulsory but would much rather have been tinkering with cars.

"Can you fix it?" asked Roger.

"Yes, Dad, but it'll take some time," his son replied from under the bonnet, "I'll take you to the match in my car."

"Your car?" said Roger horrified. "Your car's worse than mine."

"At least my car goes," his son pointed out.

Reluctantly Roger and Wally got into the old banger. The seats were torn and the suspension was virtually non-existent. No sooner had they set off than the heavens opened and it poured down. Roger shuffled in his seat to avoid the rain coming in through the broken quarterlight.

"The way this old banger's leaking, we'll drown before we get there," grumbled Roger.

"That's all right. There'll be another boat along soon," laughed Wally.

"It'll be a mud bath! Won't they call the match off in these conditions?" queried Donald.

"Nah! It's ideal for sliding tackles," quipped Wally.

When they arrived at the ground they discovered that their substitute hadn't turned up.

"This is no way to carry on," complained Roger, "he's probably still got a hangover from last night. It's just not professional, that's all."

"Look at that pitch, it's like a quagmire!" commented Donald, peering at the lake which appeared to be forming in the centre circle.

71

For this astute piece of observation, Donald was promptly awarded the dubious honour of holding the coats and jumpers. The only other spectator was a dog of uncertain origin who was more than keen to join in with the proceedings. Eventually the two rain soaked teams squelched onto the pitch and lined up to face each other. A picture of reluctance; twenty-two men without an alibi between them. As they kicked off Donald remarked to the dog.

"Look! it's the Clash of the Titans."

It's ten minutes in this exciting fixture between the Rose and Crown and The Nag's Head. Roger MacKinnon is playing a blinder. He receives a pass from teammate Wally Burnes. MacKinnon dribbles past two and sidesteps another lunging tackle. The crowd roars with excitement....

Roger is brought back to reality. No sooner had he received a pass when the Nags Head's centre-half collides with him. Roger goes down like a sack of potatoes clutching his knee. Repeated attempts with the cold, wet sponge fail to work its magic. It's obvious Roger will take no further part in this crucial match, so Wally asks Donald to take his place. Spare kit is hastily cobbled together but, alas, there are no size ten football boots to fit him. Wally earns his place in the team this week with a sudden flash of inspiration.

"What about those boots?" he asks Roger, "They're size ten."

"No one wears these boots," shouted Roger horrified, "only the great Donald MacKinnon could wear these boots."

"Now look, you burke," replied Wally, "you've always wanted him to be a footballer haven't you? Here's your chance. Just think, Donald MacKinnon, grandson of the great Donald Mackinnon, scores the winning goal!"

This vision beguiled Roger and, presently, his son took the field. With a shirt that was too small and a pair of shorts flapping round his knees, he looked anything but ready. Nevertheless this incongruous sight still stirred Roger's pride.

The Nags Head were awarded a corner and their winger went over to take it. It was a poor one, but as the goalkeeper came out, a gust of wind caught it. It hit an unsuspecting Donald MacKinnon on the back of the head and rebounded into the empty net for an own goal.

Nobody much fancied going for a drink that night. In fact nobody had much to say at all. They were all too much wrapped up in their own thoughts until Wally broke the silence.

"What a way to get relegated! What a stupid goal to give away!" he moaned. "I should have gone to the garden centre with the missus like she said. I tell you this much, don't expect to see me next season. I've had enough."

"I can think of a million and one things better to do on a Saturday," remarked Donald. "It's only a game isn't it Dad?"

Roger didn't answer. He was gazing out of the window...

It is now almost four minutes gone and Strathmuir are awarded a free kick thirty yards out from the goal line. Kirkthistle have four men in the wall as Donald MacKinnon shapes up to take the free kick. It's a swerving and viciously dipping shot and it's knocked the 'keeper into the back of the net. What a sensational goal, a hat-trick in the first four minutes.....

Every Time A Sheep Bareth He Loseth A Bite

"Oh dear! Why this car keeps stopping on me, I just don't know!" declared Daphne to herself. "I suppose I best take it to the garage. I wish Jack were still alive, he'd soon have fixed it."

She was none too pleased to receive a hefty bill from the garage.

"It needed a new carburettor and your fuel pump was u.s." claimed the mechanic. "If I were you, lady, I'd get it booked in here for a service."

"But that's what I asked you to do," cried Daphne, "a service is what I wanted."

"Yeah well, the carburettor had gone and so had the fuel pump," repeated the mechanic trying to assure her, "see the receptionist, she'll book you in."

Daphne tried to get an explanation from the mechanic for the huge bill but he neither wanted to listen or had the time. He kept repeating his claims about the carburettor and fuel pump. She wasn't disputing that, she wanted him to justify the expensive labour charges and why the car hadn't been serviced.

"Young man," she said politely, "every time a Sheep bareth he loseth a bite."

This was her favourite proverb. She used it for all kinds of situations regardless of its relevance. The mechanic ignored her and walked away.

The following day she was reading the local newspaper when an advertisement caught her eye. It read.

"Learn car maintenance in thirteen easy lessons."

"Hum," thought Daphne, "perhaps I could give it a try."

She cancelled the service with the garage and gamely set off for her first car maintenance lesson at the local college. She had to admit to being nervous, she was worried she might make a fool of herself. She needn't have worried. Most of the pupils were women like herself who had suddenly found themselves in need of this knowledge. Malcolm, the tutor, was a mild mannered young man who was teaching at the college, in his spare time, to save for a deposit to buy a house with his fiancée. To help everybody feel at ease he told the class about himself and then asked his pupils, each one in turn, to say a few words about themselves.

"My name's Mildred," announced a large lady, "I've come to learn car maintenance because I think I can do a better job than these garage mechanics. No education that's their trouble."

Daphne didn't take to this lady. She kept interrupting the lesson to question Malcolm and to assert her opinions. Daphne didn't like her aggressive manner and the way she kept complaining. Malcolm was trying to explain the basic principles of how a car worked but Mildred seemed to know better.

"Every time a Sheep bareth he loseth a bite!" exclaimed Daphne.

This outburst had succeeded in stopping Mildred talking but only for a short while.

"It is very important that you service your car regularly," Malcolm advised the class, "changing the oil is fundamental in that."

"My car needs more oil in it every week," claimed Mildred, "I don't see any need for an oil change."

"It's interesting you should say that, Mildred," replied Malcolm, "I suspect you've got a leak. Perhaps you need a new gasket."

"She needs something all right," thought Mildred, "a silencer might be more appropriate."

Mildred kept on complaining. Daphne rose to say her famous words. The rest of the class knew what was coming and joined in.

"Every time a Sheep bareth it loseth a bite!" they all shouted.

Mildred kept quiet for a while.

Even after several weeks Mildred was still interrupting class. Daphne suggested, to Malcolm, that he give the class a test on what they had learnt so far.

"It's an interesting idea, Daphne," Malcolm told her, "but I'm not sure what purpose it'll serve."

"Trust me," replied Daphne, "I don't believe Mildred has learnt a thing since classes started. A test will prove it. Every time a Sheep bareth he loseth a bite."

Malcolm laughed: "I wouldn't wish to embarrass her."

"You wouldn't need to," laughed Daphne," she's making a very good job of it by herself."

Malcolm decided to implement Daphne's idea and he read the questions to the class the following week.

"I can't see why it's necessary for us to take this test," complained Mildred.

"I just want to see what you've all learnt, that's all, Mildred," replied Malcolm.

"Well I think it's a waste of time," stated Mildred, "I shall write to the college head and tell him so."

"We'll see," Malcolm calmly replied, "when you"re all finished, I'll collect in the papers," he told the class.

The following week Malcolm read out the results from the test.

"In first place, with a ninety per cent pass, was Daphne.

The rest of the pupils applauded. Malcolm then read out the marks for the remainder of the class. Mildred sat feeling very uncomfortable, she knew

78

she hadn't faired well. Then came the moment she had been dreading. She had come last, not one question did she get right.

"I don't think this car mechanics is my cup of tea," she said sadly, "perhaps I ought to give it a miss."

"Oh don't give up," pleaded Daphne, "I'll help you learn."

Malcolm was surprised to hear Daphne say that. He had half expected her to reel in Mildred's failure. But there she was convincing Mildred to continue the lessons.

"At least I've learn one thing," smiled Mildred.

"What's that?" asked Daphne.

Mildred chuckled: "Every time a Sheep bareth he loseth a bite!"

Frank's Decision

As Frank slowly replaced the receiver that bleak February morning, he realised he would have to make a decision - one that would probably affect the rest of his life. No, not probably, definitely. If he decided to take up his mate's offer it would affect the rest of his life. And that was just the trouble. He wasn't sure if he could go through with it.

His was sick of getting up on those frosty mornings, stepping outside into the dark early morning air. His face numb, his nose running, his lips frozen, he'd make his way to the bus stop. On more than one occasion he'd slipped on the ice and almost broken his leg. More often than not the bus would be late and sometimes it never turned up. If only he could learn to drive but somehow he never got the hang of it.

How he hated his humdrum life at the office and his humdrum life at home. He yearned for the life when he was a diving instructor and when he regularly travelled the World. In those days he was single but then he met his wife, Carole and life changed from then on.

Now he did nothing but travel to and from work. His boss, Malcolm, was even fed up with him moping about.

"Why don't you get yourself a life, Frank?"

"Get myself a life?" Frank glared at Malcolm. "What street gutter language is that supposed to be?"

"You what?"

"What you mean is why don't I get myself a hobby or something."

"Wouldn't be a bad idea would it, Frank? I mean, look at me."

"Do I have to?"

"No need to be like that, Frank, just saying it for your own good you understand. Why don't you go swimming? You used to swim didn't you?"

There was no use in Frank arguing with his boss. Malcolm would always over simplify everything. Frank could never get him to understand a quick dip in a pool laced with chlorine, at some stuffy centrally heated indoor leisure complex, could never compare with deep sea diving. The coral reefs, fish of all shapes and sizes, the wonders of the sea bed. That was what life was about. Not spending eight hours a day at the marine insurance office, going home and listening to his wife ask the same silly question.

"Hello dear, had an interesting day at the office?"

"No, boring as hell," he would always reply.

So should he turn his back on all this? This meaningless existence? What sort of life was this? Thinking about it logically there could be only one answer. Whether he'd the guts to go through with it

81

was another matter. True, he'd just telephoned the airport and booked his flight to the Bahamas. No doubt he'll phone again in a minute and cancel.

Yet if he didn't go he'd be missing the opportunity of a lifetime. His mate, Tom, was working as a waiter with the Los Tros Hotel and had managed to persuade the owner to take Frank on as a diving instructor. What a wonderful life! Just spending a few hours a day teaching the holiday makers a few basic diving techniques and the rest of the day was his.

Frank was feeling guilty. It would be a rotten thing to do to Carole all said and done. Would she be able to manage? Perhaps she'd come with him? Perhaps not! The mortgage had been paid off thanks to his inheritance from Aunt Doreen. That would help, but would she be able to cope?

Stepping outside the cold wind cut through him. That decided it for Frank. He would go to the Bahamas. He knew Carole would be home late from work that evening so he could phone from the Bahamas and leave a message on the answer phone. If she wanted to follow it would be up to her.

He booked in at the airport and sat in the departure lounge. He looked out of the window and watched the snow falling. He smiled. He'd soon be bathing in the basking sun.

"Frank, I'm glad I've caught you, I was afraid I'd miss you."

Frank looked up to see Tom standing there holding two suitcases.

"Tom, what are you doing here?"

"Bad news, Frank. The Los Tros Hotel has been sold. The new owner has hired his own staff. So here I am. Afraid your job's been given to some woman. Probably some bimbo."

"But I'd made up my mind. I wasn't going home again, I was on my way to paradise."

"Nobody's more gutted than me, Frank. I'm out of job."

Shocked, Frank took a taxi to his office. His humdrum day seemed even more humdrum than usual. He resolved to go home and pretend nothing had happened but Carole wasn't there. At first he thought she'd missed the bus but on the table was a note from Carole. She wrote.

"Dear Frank.

I've had a boring as hell day for the last three years but you've been too busy wallowing in your own self pity to notice. I have had enough. By the time you read this I shall be in the Bahamas. I've got myself a job as a diving instructor at the Los Tros Hotel. If you want to follow we can start again, the way it used to be.

Remember when we first met. Both of us happy as diving instructors, travelling the World. I want that life back, Frank. With or without you. It's your decision, Frank, it's up to you.

I've reserved you a flight on the ten thirty. If you come, we'll crack open a bottle of champagne. If not, have a nice life, Frank."

Frank burst into fits of laughter. Always full of surprises was Carole. He took one last look round the room. His solicitor could take care of the details. Then he closed the door for the last time. Frank had made his decision.

Henrietta

Henrietta was desperately unhappy. Who wouldn't have been? Along with her fellow inmates she'd been condemned to captivity. Her prison was dark and dingy. There were no windows and artificial light offered her only comfort. On that day, though, she was feeling particularly sad. Her best friend, Alice, had just died. Her captors said that Alice had died of some disease. No doubt Alice did have an illness, who wouldn't have in that awful place? But Henrietta knew it wasn't the disease what killed her. Alice had given up on a world that offered no hope and she died of a broken heart.

Henrietta was heart broken at the loss of her friend. Alice could remember what life was like on the outside and Henrietta used to love hearing stories about the beautiful countryside. Scented wild flowers growing in open fields. Tall, ancient trees and scenic hills. Henrietta longed to breath in fresh air, feel the suns rays on her back, be cooled by the wind's breeze and for rain drops to refresh her face. It sounded like magic to Henrietta. But with Alice's death, Henrietta was left alone with her memories.

The captors never called Alice by name. She was merely number twenty-one to them and twenty-one was to be replaced later that morning. Or was it night time? It was difficult for Henrietta to tell the difference.

Henrietta was number twenty-two. Next to her was Mavis, number twenty- three, but twenty-three looked as if she would be joining Alice in the sky.

Henrietta was a slave to these heartless people who treated and used her like a machine. Like the others she was forced to work long hours in cramped conditions just to make her captors richer. The richer they got, the greedier they became and the harder Henrietta was forced to work.

"Productivity must increase by twenty percent," they claimed, "we must utilise the profits."

They didn't think she understood. A mere slave, a mere machine. How could she possibly have any feelings? She couldn't feel pain, could she? She knew nothing of fear, surely? Man has developed machines to remain in one place and do their job without complaint. But Henrietta wasn't a machine. She was flesh and blood. Surely her captors realised this?

Not only had they imprisoned her physical being, they'd also imprisoned her mind and soul. Why hadn't they shown her some compassion? If only they'd looked into her tragic eyes, observed her lifeless body and noticed the cuts and bruises on her feet. But they were making a profit so what did it matter?

When Henrietta had first arrived her captors regarded her as a good worker. In fact, they were enormously pleased. A few more like her and the profits would have soon risen. They'd hoped to get a few good years out of her but the appalling conditions had left their mark. Her productivity deteriorated with the passage of time and eventually her captors looked upon her as a liability.

"She'll have to go, she's not pulling her weight. We'll send her off with the other clapped out females tomorrow. In fact, one of the males is no good to us now. I'll put him on the lorry too."

Henrietta knew what this meant. For those who went on the lorry their captors had devised a horrifying method of execution. They cut the inmates throats and as their blood eased out of their bodies, they were left to die a slow painful death. Oh yes, she knew what it meant all right.

She'd spent the last few hours on death row restless, wondering when the lorry would come? Wondering what might have been? Wondering what it was like to live her life as a free spirit? These thoughts tortured her mind throughout the night but her execution would put an end to her misery.

She pitied her captors. How anyone could put profit before life mystified her. Before she'd died, Alice had told her about those who were wonderful, kind and compassionate. Many dedicated their lives for the cause. Even when it meant being outcast by others, they had stuck to their principles. Henrietta would have loved to have met one of these people but she'd known only of a dark side to humanity.

Surely they could have lived in harmony with each other?

The time came. Henrietta was bundled onto the lorry along with other unfortunate inmates. It was a new experience for her travelling in the back of a lorry. She was bumped and bounced about and she was very frightened. A handsome male called Alec comforted her. She looked into his eyes and it was love at first sight. Suddenly she was no longer afraid. Her Knight In Shinning Armour was with her. They would hold each other tight until their dying breath.

Some say it was the band of Animal Rights Protesters who caused the accident. More likely the driver had lost control whilst trying to steer and make a call with his mobile phone.

The protesters, perhaps to their discredit, didn't rush to help him. It wouldn't have made any difference, though, he died instantly when the lorry tipped on its back. Instead the protesters had opened the lorry's rear doors and released all the chickens who had survived the crash.

Amongst them was Henrietta and her new found love, Alec. The protesters' banners were waived in triumph. "Anti Battery Farm Eggs" slogans were chanted.

Henrietta was in a terrible state when she was placed, along with Alec, in the kind hands of Ron and Sarah. Gradually with their medical care and Alec's love, she eventually made a full recovery.

She now lives on a small holding where the animals are free to roam and where Henrietta can live a full and natural life.

Alec is as proud as any cock could be. One of Henrietta's eggs hatched and produced a bouncing baby chick. Henry is his mother's pride and joy.

He's No Friend Of Mine

"He's no friend of mine, I tell you".

I've been saying this over and over again. For hours and hours. He just won't listen. Why won't he listen?

Inspector MacBride doesn't believe a word I'm saying. He's losing his patience. Any minute now he's going to let loose his gorilla on me who's posing as a Sergeant. This gorilla, I notice amongst other things, has massive hands and his fists are clenched at the ready. Now I know it's 1950 and police brutality should be a thing of the past but you hear about these things, don't you? I mean you just don't know what he might do if MacBride lets him. I look around the interrogation room. There are no windows. The light is dingy save the bright light aimed directly at my face. I'm feeling very scared right now.

MacBride is investigating a bank robbery and he knows Laurence Smythe is behind it all but he can't prove it. Never been able to prove anything against Smythe. Responsible for a hundred or more crimes but Smythe is too clever. So MacBride is taking it out on me. He's hoping I will tell him something which might lead to Smythe's arrest but I know nothing.

"Look, Inspector MacBride," I say pleading. "I know Laurence Smythe, can't deny it but please believe me, he's no friend of mine".

MacBride says nothing for a minute, just stands there glaring. His eyes on fire, his jaws locked, his face disapproving. His fists clenched. He slams the table. His coffee cup jumps off the saucer momentarily and then lands again. The saucer and cup are reunited.

"It's only a matter of time son and you'll crack. May as well make it easy on yourself. Get it off your chest, it'll make you feel better. Cooperate and I see what I can do. First offence. Judge could go easy on you, if you confess".

"But I haven't done anything. You must believe me, Inspector MacBride."

"Don't tell me what I must do, you little wimp. I'll be the judge in this case and the evidence suggests to me you're lying."

"I'm not lying. I'm innocent."

I bow my head in despair. I rub fingers across my eyes. I'm weary. My mind searches for an alibi but I have none I can prove. I was alone in my flat when the crime was committed and there's no one to verify my story. I fear the worse. I fear I will be sent to prison for something I didn't do and all because I know Laurence Smythe. Yet at least half the people in London know Laurence Smythe but they're not being questioned. They're not being accused.

MacBride is such an ass but I daren't tell him so. I'm in enough trouble already.

"I tell you what I think," MacBride says almost casually, "I think you're on Smythe's payroll.

"No, you're mistaken Inspector MacBride." I cry desperately trying to convince him.

"Then what were you doing at his house only days before the robbery?"

"I've told you."

"Tell me again."

So I go over my story again. Two of Smythe's goons turn up at my flat and say he wants to see me. Well, I wasn't going to argue with those brutes so I go with them. They take me to see Smythe and he offers me a job but I politely refuse. I tell him I have a job and I'm happy with it. I'm shaking with fear when I say this.

"So why should Smythe offer you a job?" MacBride demands to know.

"I've explained that."

"Explain it again."

I sigh and tell MacBride for at least the fourth time about the night I inadvertently saved Smythe's life. There was I driving along Oxford Street late one evening, I'd been visiting friends and had stayed longer than intended. There isn't a soul about as I drive along with the rain hammering against the windscreen, my wipers at full speed, I keep wiping the glass to stop it from misting up. In front of me is a diversion sign and I've no choice but to go down this side street. I no longer know where I am as I follow the diversion signs and you know what it's like. Just when I need a diversion sign there's no more. I try to get back on track but end up getting hopelessly lost. I find myself driving down a narrow street and that's when it happens.

I see a couple of thugs kicking the hell out of this man by the side of the road. I'm not a brave man in the least but instinctively I drive towards these thugs, I rev the engine, my headlights on full beam, I sound my horn. It works and the thugs flea the scene. I stop the car and the badly beaten man scrambles to his feet and gets in my car and occupies the passenger seat. I soon learn that he's Smythe.

"Drive!" Smythe commands.

I suggest to Smythe I take him to the nearest hospital and call the police but he'll have none of it. Instead he barks his directions. "Turn left, turn right, go straight on." If I'd any clue where I was before I've none now. I'm new to London and I don't know my way round very well. I stop outside a posh private house in a posh street but I know where not. I help Smythe out of the car, blood still pouring down his face, we scramble to the door and I knock hard. A man comes to the door and we go inside. This man seems to me to be a doctor and attends to Smythe's injuries. It's soon decided Smythe will stay the night and I take the earliest opportunity to leave but not before Smythe has slipped fifty quid into my top pocket. I daren't refuse it. Somehow I find my way home. A week later Smythe has tracked me down and has sent for me.

"Didn't you twig he was villain?" MacBridge asks rather credulously.

"Of course I did but it was too late by then. Anyway he said he was indebted to me for saving his life. I didn't want to accept the fifty quid but he insisted. You don't argue with a man like that."

"Didn't it occur to you he might have given you stolen money?"

"He assured me it wasn't stolen."

"He assured you!"

MacBride starts to laugh. There's even a chuckle from the gorilla.

"That's all right then, isn't it? Smythe assured you the money wasn't stolen! I can't quite work out if it's you that's naïve or if you think I am? Even if the actual notes he gave you weren't stolen the money's not honest money."

"No, you're right Inspector MacBride. I shouldn't have taken the money but I was too scared not to."

"What did you do with that fifty quid?"

"Paid some bills, bought some clothes. I bought a new suit. Needed that for work."

"Well, I hope you can sleep at night." MacBride says with some disgust. "So why tell him your name and where you live?"

94

"What would you have done Inspector MacBride? When someone asks you your name it's very difficult not to tell them. Anyway he wasn't threatening me so I told him. I thought he would have forgotten it by the morning or least I hoped he would. I tried to be as vague as I could about where I lived but he tracked me down. He did seem genuinely grateful to me for saving his life."

"There's nothing genuine about Smythe. Except that he's a genuine crook. The thing is," MacBride began pacing up and down, "the thing is I've got a problem with at least some of your story. Okay, there was a diversion in Oxford Street that night so I'll accept your explanation for that. I'll even except you got lost and being dark you probably wouldn't have been able to see any street signs. I'll even buy your story about you helping him when he was being attacked and yeah he's probably got a few doctors on his payroll."

"I don't understand then, surely you're saying you believe me?" I ask puzzled.

"No, you see, I have a problem with the rest of your story. You see I think he recruited you that night when he discovered you work for a bank. The same bank that was robbed recently and I believe you were his inside man. Being an employee of the bank would have made you very useful to Smythe."

"It's not true, I tell you. I'm innocent, really I am Inspector MacBride."

"Then why is it someone fitting your description was seen moments later driving away at speed from the scene of the crime? You see my point, don't you? So why don't you just confess and stop wasting my time."

I had to see it from MacBride's point of view. It wasn't looking good for me but he had no proof. I kept telling myself this. He had no proof because I've done nothing wrong except perhaps I shouldn't have accepted that fifty quid but then if I hadn't Smythe might have got nasty and killed me.

I'm now certain in my mind now is the time when MacBride is going to set his gorilla on me. The gorilla is itching to have a crack at me. Then at this moment a well dressed man, wearing glasses and carrying a suitcase bursts into the room.

MacBride turns to this man: "I was wondering when you would show up."

The man with the glasses calmly asks MacBride: "Are you going to charge my client?"

"He's helping us with our enquiries."

"Either charge my client or we're leaving." Glasses demands.

MacBride's face is red with rage. He kicks a chair. It bounces and rolls across the room.

"Get out of here." MacBride shouts. "I've got your card marked. Make one mistake and I'll have you."

His warning is clearly aimed at me. I soon discover that Glasses is Smythe's solicitor. Glasses gives me some advice.

"Mr Smythe now considers you're even. He's no longer in your debt for saving his life although he'll always be grateful to you. I suggest you take this opportunity to get out of town, far away from here. Mr Smythe wishes you all the best."

Glasses hands me an envelope. An envelope full of fivers. Not stolen he emphasises.

"What about MacBride?" I ask.

"He won't come after you. Just make sure he never sees you again."

I then go to my flat and take Glasses advice or Smythe's orders more like. I pack my suitcase, pay the landlord all the rent I owe and take the first train out of London. I send my employer a letter of apology for quitting without notice. I write it's for personal reasons but I don't elaborate.

A year has passed and I'm sat reading a newspaper. I'm a hundred miles from London and I've got myself another job and another place to stay. I read in the newspaper that Smythe's trial for the bank job collapses due to a lack of evidence. MacBride will be fuming! But who cares? He's no friend of mine.

If Only

If only we'd said goodbye... If only things were different... If only I'd understood... If only...

I remember you, as if it were yesterday, standing in the function hall, a glass of mineral water in hand. I'll never forget that, it was your favourite tipple, aside from a very weak mug of tea. Now that makes me smile. I shall always remember fondly, it had to be a mug and not a cup. You were always very particular about your tea, weren't you!

The tea bag was placed in the mug but as soon as it met with hot water it was immediately scooped out with a spoon. There wasn't a moment to lose if a strong mug of tea was to be avoided. And that's how you always drank it - weak - no milk - no sugar.

When we were first introduced we began chatting about this and that. We became so engrossed in conversation we'd successfully blocked out all that was happening around us. The disco beat thudded in the other room but it failed to capture our attention.

I remember boldly suggesting a dinner-date to get to know each other and to my delight you readily agreed. Odd as it may sound, perhaps because I didn't kiss you afterwards, I'd become more attracted to you?

We met again for a picnic with some friends. Like children we played rounders and cheered our side onto victory. Afterwards we went for stroll in the park and later climbed the tower to view the magnificent countryside. That evening we walked alongside the river bank and watched as one or two barges chugged slowly by. Then, for the first time, we kissed.

I was thrilled when you said you would like to come on holiday with me. I'd packed my car solid with bits and pieces just about leaving enough room for the both of us. We happily sped off on our adventure as the sun came out to honour the day.

We stopped for lunch at a motorway cafe. You drank your usual weak tea whilst I sipped a cup of coffee. It may have been my imagination but I felt you didn't approve. You would never drink it but I didn't like the taste of tea.

We enjoyed our holiday. I was a little surprised when you sunbathed topless but to you it seemed the natural thing to do. The sun was too hot for me; I sought protection in the shade but you never understood that. If anything, you disapproved.

Your doubts concerning our relationship submerged towards the end of the holiday but I managed to temporally ease them. A game was in the making, one in which I couldn't win. The months ahead saw me as the salesman trying desperately to sell me to you - us to you! You became the prospective buyer but was never going to buy.

I held your hand, tenderly, one evening, as we watched a play at the local theatre. I was ill-prepared for when you told me it was all over between us. We were too different; we didn't have enough in common you concluded.

I protested. We were both vegetarians, enjoyed going to the theatre, liked to walk in the countryside. You quickly pointed out that you were the vegetarian, I was a vegan. Yes, we both liked the theatre but we'd different reasons for liking to walk in the countryside, you argued. And let's not forget: I liked coffee. You liked tea.

I didn't give up, I continued to air my point of view. Somehow I managed to persuade you that our relationship was, at least, worth further consideration. So you agreed to think it over and commented that I was a good salesman. Was that a compliment or a twisted criticism?

That night I didn't sleep very well but I awoke the morning with my mind made up. I wrote and thanked you for the time we had together, there was no point in prolonging the agony, it would be best to let you go.

I was astounded when you replied begging me not to end it between us. Surely that's what you wanted! Why had you seemingly changed your mind? I should have been strong and stuck to my guns. But I couldn't help myself, we met again and for a while it was wonderful between us.

Inevitably our relationship was soon hanging by a thread. We saw less and less of each other. I was forced to admit, to myself, that I would never mean anything to you. I simply couldn't make it like the movies; those violins would never play.

Christmas Day came and it was to be the final performance for us. Until then, there'd been a number of dress rehearsals but this time we knew this was it. There'd be no more goodbyes, no spoken regrets or tears to shed. You'd struck with the killer punch, it was a blow I just couldn't take.

I blame myself. I blame you. I blame us. We failed in someway but I will never know why. If only I could have made you happy... If only we'd talked more... If only I'd liked tea or you coffee... If only...

Impossible Choice

David was asleep in his bedroom when he was awakened by loud voices from downstairs. He could hear his father's voice, the other two me he wasn't sure of.

David was twenty-two years of age; the son of an East London gang leader. His father ran a protection racket and a couple of his own night clubs. A feud between his gang, The Pickfords and his deadly rivals, The Greenwoods, had been boiling up for some time. It had started up over a futile argument in an Eastend Pub many years ago. The leader of the Greenwoods, Norman Greenwood, was an evil middle aged man who would kill his own mother for capital gain. Ronald Pickford had grown to hate him. He had sent word for Greenwood to come to his house to warn him to keep away from his patch.

The shouting grew louder and louder. David heard the sound of a gunshot followed by the screeching noise of car wheels racing away. He rushed downstairs to find his father dead on the lounge floor. Nothing could have prepared him for seeing his own father lying there but somehow he felt strangely relieved. He had hated being the son of a villain and had often quarrelled with him. The moment his father's estate was settled he would be free to start a new life.

At the funeral Norman Greenwood was there to offer his insincere condolences.

"So sorry about your father," he grinned at David, "Too bad he messed with the wrong sort of people."

"Yes, too bad, wasn't it," replied David nonchalantly. "He mixed with a lot of rotten scum. Some he liked, some he didn't. The trouble with Dad was he got sloppy. It's no good when you get to be sloppy, is it Norman? You make it easy for others to move in don't you Norman?"

"Tut, tut, you wouldn't be threatening me would you?" Norman snapped. "Nobody threatens me."

Norman left with two other members of his gang, Johnny Shepherd and Tosh Day. These three were the most evil and feared men in London.

David started to receive threatening phone calls and anonymous notes. At first he took little notice, but one day, as he walked down a street, a car came hurtling towards him. He froze on the spot, but in the nick of time was pulled out of the way and saved from certain death.

"Thanks, I owe you my life," he said to the tramp who had pulled him clear.

"That's all right," said the tramp, "anything to thwart Norman Greenwood," as his face filled with rage.

"Who are you?" asked David. "How do you know he was responsible for that? What do you know about him?"

"Grant's my name," he replied. "I've got Norman Greenwood to thank for these rags. I used to have a nice little life until he came along with his protection racket. He destroyed my business and left for me dead," he fought back the tears, "but one day he'll get careless."

David hardly knew what to say. The tramp regained his composure.

"What's he after you for?"

"He killed my father, now I suppose he wants to kill me," replied David, trying to understand why Greenwood was after him.

"Haven't you gone to the police," asked the tramp.

David laughed: "The police are only too glad my father's dead. You see, my father was no better than his killer. I'm David Pickford. My father was Ronald Pickford. A crook just like Norman Greenwood," he bowed his head in shame.

"Yes," said the tramp nodding his head. "I've heard of your father. You obviously didn't like him."

"I hated him," David said passionately. "I hated his evil life." He clenched his fist tightly as he began to shake.

The tramp stood and looked at David for a few moments: "If I were in your shoes, I'd get as far away from here as possible. I know Norman Greenwood. He won't take any chances. He'll want you out of the way just in case you try to avenge your father's death."

"Where can I go?" asked David. "My mother's dead. I've no family except for a second cousin who lives in a village called Wint in Essex. I've not seen her for about fifteen years."

The tramp looked at him: "Then it's about time you renewed your acquaintance."

David went home, packed his bags and left the house never to return. Soon he was on the train to Essex and would seek out his second cousin, Anna, in the village of Wint. He was glad to get away. He could start a new life for himself, away from the violence and dishonesty his father had left in his wake. Yet David felt guilty and annoyed with himself that he hadn't stayed to stand up to Norman Greenwood. This man was evil and deserved the worst.

Meanwhile Greenwood and his men had come looking for David. They forced entry into his house smashing everything as they searched top to bottom for him.

"Where's he gone?" barked Greenwood.

"Let's leave it. He obviously ran away," said Tosh Day. "He won't be bothering us."

"Never let it be said, Norman Greenwood doesn't finish a job. So find him we will. Then, we kill him," replied Greenwood.

"But Norm', you could be making a great mistake. He's probably out of London by now," advised Johnny Shepherd, "you're amongst friends here."

"Johnny's right," continued Tosh. "It could be dangerous to leave the manor. We could be vulnerable."

"Listen, you two," shouted Greenwood as he grabbed both of them by the scruff of their necks. "I promised my father, God rest his soul, that I'd wipe out the Pickford family. Every single one of them. He knows I killed his father and he knows that I'm going to come and kill him."

"You're a nutter," replied Tosh, "David Pickford's no threat to you."

"I don't care about that. He's a Pickford and he must die."

David arrived in Wint just at it started to rain. He sought shelter in the local pub, The Green Dragon and bought a pint of beer. It was a very old pub with genuine oak beams and an atmosphere that could only be experienced in a village local. David began to enquire about his cousin Anna. Nobody responded to his questions until an old lady, sitting in the corner of the bar suddenly spoke. She had a shawl wrapped around her and was sipping half a stout.

"I think I be knowing who yer looking for," her eyes gazing up at him.

"Do you?" replied David excitedly. "Where can I find her?"

"All in good time," she said deviously, "but first another bottle of stout," holding out her empty glass to David.

David bought her another drink and sat beside her.

"That be very kind of you," she said, "good of you to look after an old lady. Cheers!"

"Cheers," replied David, "Anna? You know where I can find Anna?"

"Now that depends on which Anna you be looking for," she replied teasing him. "There's Anna Brown the milkman's wife, Anna Smith who runs the stables. Anna Dorking, no it wouldn't be her, she's ninety three..."

"I'm looking for Anna Metcalf," interrupted David rather impatiently, "she's about my age."

She replied: "Well depending on what age you are..."

"Look do you know her or not?" demanded David.

The old woman laughed: "Sure, you'll find her at Metcalf farm on top of the hill."

"Thanks," said David as he picked up his coat.

David made his way steadily up the hill to Metcalf farm. The rain had stopped by now but it had left behind a few puddles and made walking a bit slippery. His mind wandered back to his home in London. Was it the right thing to do to run away?

Perhaps he should have stayed and sorted things out with Greenwood. His mind was tormenting him with these questions. No, he thought, you can't reason with a man like Greenwood. He had no choice but to run away. What if Greenwood comes looking for him? What would he do then? No. Greenwood wouldn't leave London. He wouldn't go to that much trouble. After all, who was David? The son of Ronald Pickford that's what.

He walked around the farmyard hoping to find Anna. It was a small farm but with an obvious abundance of vegetables and other crops. He knocked at the door, his heart began to beat faster. He could hear the sound of footsteps drawing nearer to him down the quarry tiled passage way. The door opened. David drew a deep breath. There, standing in the doorway was Anna, she was smiling, her beautiful dark hair and rosy cheeks were a sight to behold.

"Can I help you?" she inquired.

"Anna," he replied, "Anna Metcalf?"

"Yes," she answered, I'm sorry I..."

"It's David, your second cousin," he interrupted.

Anna looked puzzled.

"David Pickford. Don't you remember me?" he persisted.

"David!" she suddenly realised who he was. "What a surprise. I haven't seen you for years.

Haven't you changed! You used to be all spotty and pale faced," she laughed. "Come on in."

He told her about his father and Norman Greenwood. She listened to him sympathetically and was happy for him to stay. She assured him he had done the right thing by leaving London. Besides, another pair of hands would be welcome on the farm, particularly as the potatoes were ready for picking.

Once day he was gathering hay in the barn and Anna had climbed to the top. She walked precariously along the ledge.

"Be careful, Anna," warned David.

"I'm all right," she insisted, "don't fuss so."

Suddenly she lost her balance and fell ten feet into the haystack. David rushed into it in a blind panic only to find Anna lying there giggling. He started to laugh too.

"You silly girl, I told you to be more careful," he said, trying to sound serious, but couldn't keep a straight face. They laughed until their sides ached. Then, Anna reached out and pulled him into the haystack. As their eyes drew nearer, they embraced one another and their lips met again and again. They realised they had fallen in love.

From that day on they were devoted lovers. They planned their wedding which was to be held at the local church. It would be a small affair; just a few friends from the village would attend. An ex–boyfriend of Anna's, Roger Scriven, was very jealous of her new found love and happiness. She had ended their relationship after finding out he was nothing more than a liar and a thief. He had served three years in prison but had told her that he had been away at sea. He started to pester her every time she went to the village. She should have told David but didn't want to cause any unpleasantness.

Scriven followed her back to her farm one day. He saw that David was out ploughing a field and stole inside the house.

"Get out," shouted Anna. "You've no right to be here."

"Just want to talk. No harm in that is there?" he said menacingly.

"I've nothing to say to you. Now get out before David finds you here," she demanded.

"Not very friendly are you," his evil eye gazing at her. "You didn't used to be like this."

Scriven pulled Anna to the floor but he then received a thump on the back his neck which felled him. He got to his feet and fled. Anna got up from the floor sobbing as she did so she caught sight of a scruffy looking man leaving the house. She didn't know who he was but it must have been him who had saved her from the terrible ordeal. She'd seen some strange people coming through the village from time to time but she'd never set eyes on this character before.

David went to the police and Scriven was arrested, but later released on bail. He was forbidden to go near Anna.

Norman Greenwood arrived at the village pub with his two associates. They began asking questions about David. Scriven was there perched on a bar stool.

"I know where you can find him," he told Greenwood.

"What yer drinking?" Greenwood asked him.

"Scotch. Double Scotch," he replied.

"A double Scotch for my friend here," Greenwood ordered to the barman. "Now tell me," he asked Scriven. "Where can I find David Pickford?"

"I only know his name's David. We're only on first name terms you see," he laughed sarcastically.

Greenwood and his two associates just looked blankly at him.

"Look here, matey, I'm not in the mood. Just tell me where I can find him", snarled Greenwood.

"You'll find him at the farm on top of the hill," quivered Scriven.

David was in the yard with Anna when Greenwood and his two companions arrived.

"Well, well, well. David Pickford has gone Green," mocked Greenwood. "Your father would be proud."

"I don't care what my father would have thought," replied David angrily.

"Who are these people?" asked Anna.

"Beg pardon, darling," said Greenwood lifting his hat. "I'm Greenwood. My two business associates, Johnny Shepherd and Tosh Day."

Shepherd and Day lifted their hats but said nothing.

"David's told me all about you Mr Greenwood. He wants nothing to do with your world. You've no business here," she told him.

"Oh, very grand. Here that, boys? David Pickford's gone up in the world. Too good for us now are you, Pickford?" Greenwood said fiercely.

"Just say your piece, Greenwood and take your monkeys with you," demanded David unwisely.

"I'm a fair sort of a guy," said Greenwood. "I'm going to give you a choice."

"The same choice you gave my father," retorted David.

"Oh! very quick," laughed Greenwood. "Very quick isn't he boys. Very witty. You can stand there while we shoot you, or you can run and we'll still shoot you. Now which way's it going to be?"

"You always offer an impossible choice, don't you, Greenwood," said David bitterly. "I wouldn't have expected anything more from you. That's the sort of man you are, the deals only on when you're holding all the aces."

"Leave him, please don't kill him. He's done you no harm," pleaded Anna.

"Oh very touching. Out of the way you stupid tart or I'll kill you too," shouted Greenwood as he pulled a gun from his pocket.

Anna screamed. Greenwood pointed his gun at David. The sound of gunshot rang out. Greenwood's eyes bulged, blood poured from his head as his face thudded against the mud. Before Shepherd and Tosh could retaliate they received the same fate as Greenwood. As all three lay dead on the ground, Anna screamed and hugged David tightly. David looked over his shoulder. Standing there with a shotgun still smouldering was the tramp who had previously saved David's life from Greenwood's wheels.

"It's taken ten years, Greenwood," he said calmly, "but today you finally got careless."

The Inheritance **

Liam drove slowly into the quiet village of Norman's Cross. If bricks and mortar could speak, what stories these houses could tell, some of them had stood since the early Middle Ages. His map was spread open on the passenger seat but he was unsure of quite where to go next.

"I'm looking for Godsacre, can you help me, please?" he asked some villagers.

"Nobody lives there," one of them replied. "You're not from round here, are you?"

Liam announced: "My Great Uncle Mortimer recently died and he left me Godsacre."

Not a flicker of emotion registered on the villager's face and his companions' hostile indifference made Liam feel embarrassed. Liam took the left fork in the road which lead him through winding hedgerows and passed a cluster of cottages, before he stopped his car to check his map.

Getting out of his car he gazed across at the tall wrought iron gates, which were almost overgrown with ivy. Heaving against them they grated and groaned in protest. To his surprise, instead of the neglected wilderness he'd expected, there lay before him a closely cropped field.

On his map it had indicated that this was the site of an old Nunnery and he wondered if there were still any ruins. Deep in thought, he was startled to feel a hand of restraint on his shoulder. His burly figure wheeled round to see a frail old woman standing before him.

"Can I help you?" she asked.

"Yes, perhaps you can," he replied. "I tried asking for some directions in the village but they weren't very helpful."

"Don't you take any notice of those three old fools, my dear, they're suspicious of everyone that comes to Godsacre. They don't like outsiders, you see, but you're welcome to stay, if you want to."

"I understand that a Nunnery once stood on this site," he remarked.

"Oh, yes my dear, it stood over there. See my house on top of the hill, it was once owned by the Nunnery," she pointed northwards. "Have you just moved into the village?"

"No," he replied. "I've inherited this land and I hope to build a home for myself on it."

She gave him a long thoughtful look: "I wouldn't do that, if I were you, you might upset the residents."

He strode to the middle of the field to get a better lie of the land. When he turned round the old woman had vanished.

He was feeling very pleased with himself. In no time at all, it seemed, he'd begun the foundations for his house. It had been a pleasant surprise to him to have gained planning permission at such short

115

notice. He was puzzled by the lack of resistance from the locals after what the old woman had said.

With enthusiasm, he arrived to begin a days work bricklaying. He was angered to discover that some of his tools and materials were either missing or damaged.

"Is there something wrong, dear?" It was the old woman again.

"Somebody's been at my tools and just look at all this mess. Yobbos, no doubt, with nothing better to do," he complained bitterly.

"Do you think it will delay you for very long?" she asked drily.

He sighed: "I shall just have to roll up my sleeves and get on with it, I suppose. I'm not going to be intimidated by anyone."

"Just take care, my dear. Local thugs may be the least of your worries," she cautioned.

He returned to his car for a bag of cement he'd bought from the builders merchant. When he returned the old woman had disappeared. He'd decided to work without a break to make up for lost time. That evening he resolved to keep watch, in his car, to catch the yobbos red handed.

At some point he must have dropped off to sleep because the next thing he was aware of was the morning sun streaming through the car windscreen. He stretched out his arms, yawned and decided to press on with another days work.

To his horror he stood at the site unable to believe his eyes. The area was covered in close cropped grass exactly the same as the day he'd first seen it.

"I did try to warn you," the old woman pointed at him, "bad luck will befall those who interfere. Baron Lyndhurst once owned this land. He was forced to sell it after series of disasters. His business interests overseas failed after several of his ships were lost at sea. Before he could recover from this, a mysterious illness wiped out all his livestock. If that wasn't enough, he suffered a fall from his carriage which was never properly explained. He had to abandon his plans to build a house on this land for his family."

Angry, frustrated, Liam made his way to the village and called in at the local for a consoling pint. The Landlord could see that Liam was down-in-the-dumps and befriended him.

"Cheer up, lad, it may never happen," the Landlord told him.

"It already has," Liam replied dejectedly. "Somebody, somewhere, doesn't like me. What's so special about Godsacre?"

"Oh, are you the bloke who's been building up there?" the Landlord inquired. "You're wasting your time you know. Godsacre is cursed."

Liam demanded an explanation. The Landlord continued.

"It all happened at the time of the Dissolution. They razed the Nunnery to the ground and the last Mother Superior was hounded to her death. In her pain and anguish she vowed that the Holy Ground would never be wrested from the Church. Since that day, no lay person has ever been able to hang onto Godsacre. The land is no good to nobody."

"You sound just like that old woman that lives on the hill," Liam commented.

The Landlord had been in the village for ten years or more but had never heard of this old woman or any house on the hill. Liam took the Landlord outside to point it out to him. Liam looked up and in disbelief, the old woman's house was no longer there.

"What did this old woman look like? inquired the Landlord. "Did she look like her?" he asked pointing to a portrait on the wall inside the pub.

"Yes, that's her," Liam replied in amazement, "who is she?"

"That is the last Mother Superior," the Landlord grinned.

Legend Of The Bosmoor Mist **

They had been looking forward so much to their holiday and finally that time had arrived. Leon was at the hotel to greet them all - a United Nations of holiday makers. Leon was a fit man in his sixties; he loved the countryside and telling his favourite yarns. He described, with enthusiasm, the routes they would walk over the coming week.

Amongst the holiday makers were a Dutch and German family, two Americans and four British. Unhappily, Kate, one of the American's had suffered with angina but was determined to stay the course for the week. A number of them were of retirement age, some were walking enthusiasts, unlike Michelle, the young Dutch girl who was only there because her father, Robbie, had insisted on her coming. Leon had surmised that walking along English footpaths was not Michelle's idea of a good time, but he soon discovered that, like him, she had a good sense of fun.

"We'll be walking on the moor tomorrow, where I warn you the weather can be very misty and bleak." Leon advised the party. "It leads me to tell you all about the Legend of the Bosmoor Mist." He chuckled. "Now I must make it clear that I don't necessarily believe these stories I just tell them." His face then looked very serious. "Legend has it, that if it becomes misty on Bosmoor you must be very careful not to walk in a westerly direction. For if you do and you walk between the Two Tors, you will find that the mist will quickly disappear and give way to bright sunshine. The snag is, legend has it, you will find that you have walked back in time to the Bronze Age. Some folk do say, that if you try to retrace your steps, you will age about seventy years." He then burst out laughing. "Most people never live to tell the tale!"

The next morning it was a bright sunny day as Leon led his team to the moor. Michelle was wearing a very distinctive bright red sweatshirt and matching trousers. No sooner had they reached the moor than it started to cloud over. Leon stopped to show them some evidence of Bronze Age Man. He described how they would cut into rocks with primitive tools. As the party climbed towards the highest point on the moor, the mist came over very thick.

"Keep close to me," he ordered. "I don't want anyone getting lost, not least on the first day," he smiled.

The weather worsened and visibility was down to about ten yards. Suddenly there was a cry from Robbie.

"Leon, Leon. I don't know where Michelle is. She was with me one moment. Then she vanished!"

"All right keep calm, we'll soon find her," Leon assured him. "Everyone stand still, we've lost Michelle."

They all chatted nervously. Where had she gone they were all muttering.

"Okay, everyone keep silent, please," Leon asked, "Michelle, Michelle," he called out, "where are you?"

"I'm over here," Michelle shouted back, "where did you go to?"

Everyone was much relieved to hear her voice, none more so than her father.

"All right, Michelle," called out Leon, "stay where you are. We'll come and get you."

Leon led them towards the sound of Michelle's voice. He checked his compass and noted that they were walking in a westerly direction.

"I'm the other side of the mist," she called out, "it's great here, it's really sunny. Hey, Leon, you didn't tell us about the settlement on top of the hill."

"Yes I did," Leon replied, "don't you remember? Earlier, when we were walking up, I was telling you all about the Bronze Age remains!"

"Remains! What remains?" she shouted. "It looks like a complete village to me.

"Leon looked at his map, something was wrong.

"Are you sure, Michelle?" he asked." What about the monument I was telling you about? That should be very close to you."

"Can't see a monument," she replied.

"Stop playing games, Michelle," her father shouted.

"I'm not playing games," she insisted, "there is no monument here."

"What about the wind farm?" Leon asked.

"What wind farm?" she replied.

"You must be able to see the wind farm. Look to the south of you," Leon shouted to her.

"I definitely can't see a wind farm," Michelle insisted.

"Michelle, have you walked between the Two Tors?" asked her father.

"What, you mean those big hills?" she replied, "yes I remember walking between them."

Robbie started to panic, which in turn effected the rest of the group, although Kate was grateful for a rest.

"Just calm down," demanded Leon, "there must be a simple explanation for this. Your imagination's are getting the better of you."

There was an uneasy silence. Suddenly it was broken by Michelle's raucous laughter.

"I'm sorry, it was just a joke," laughed Michelle as she rejoined the group.

Leon was furious: "Don't you ever do that again young lady. The moor is a very dangerous place. Your foolish behaviour has cost us precious time. The weather's getting worse, so I must urge you all to stick closely together. Now let's press on."

The mist was worse than Leon could ever remember. He checked his compass once again which confirmed that they were still heading west.

He was concerned that Kate was feeling the effects of the walk. They really should have been heading back by now but Leon was uncertain of their exact whereabouts.

They were all relieved when the mist cleared and gave way to bright sunshine. Leon paused and waited for the slower members to catch up. Kate arrived complaining that her angina was giving her cause for concern. Leon tried to reassure her that it wouldn't be long before they were back at the hotel and she would then be able to rest. Having taken a quick head count he realised that Michelle was missing.

"Where's Michelle gone? I hope this isn't another of her games!"

"I don't know where she is, Leon; I thought she was with you." Robbie replied. "She said she was going to catch you up. She was getting impatient with me walking so slowly."

"I haven't seen her," declared Leon, "we'll have to go back and find her."

Leon led them back towards the way they came. From a distance they could see a person in a bright red outfit on the other side of the Two Tors.

"Look, there's Michelle!" cried Robbie, "she looks lost." He ran off towards her.

Suddenly Kate was gasping for breath as she lay on the ground. Leon went to her aid and began to loosen her collar.

"My pills, my pills," she gasped.

"Where are they?" Leon asked anxiously.

"In my right jacket pocket," she muttered, "give me two, can you."

He handed her the pills and thankfully after a few minutes she began to feel better.

Leon had asked the rest of the party to take care of Kate and to catch up with Robbie whilst he looked around. As he looked, nothing made sense. He knew the wind farm should be clearly visible on this side of the Two Tors. He walked around the hill and there, to his disbelief, instead of the remains he expected to see, stood a complete Bronze Age village.

Reeling away in shock he returned to the rest of the group to find a distraught Robbie on his knees in tears. Leon placed his hand on Robbie's shoulder.

"Tell me it isn't true," cried Robbie.

"If it isn't Michelle, who is it?" replied Leon.

"Don't you think a father wouldn't know his own daughter?" sobbed Robbie.

Leon looked across the divide and saw the image of Michelle. Her hair was now thin and grey, with the wrinkled face of a woman of eighty years or more. She slowly turned and walked away, but as Leon surveyed the other members of the party, he realised that, for them, there could be no return.

Morchester's Blade *

If ye should read this whilst I still live then you will know what must have happened. If ye should read this when I am gone then have pity on my soul.

My stomach churned as I dug deep, turning the wet earth over and over. I must look at her for the last time if I am to rid myself of this guilt. Oh foolish heart! I was no match for the Earl of Morchester's power, money and good looks. I have a cursed countenance and could have never won her favour.

I loved her so. I had loved Mary MacDonald since we were children. It had always been my dearest wish that we should marry and raise a family, but my duty to God and His Ministry has never faltered.

Six forlorn months have passed since I last saw her. The fields are empty and few men have survived the scourge of the plague. No tithes are paid and the families must suffer. I was called to the Thomas house that night to administer the sacrament of last rites and was kept with them in their sorrow.

As I stepped into the darkness, I was only a few paces from their door, when I was startled by the sound of voices. I caught sight of her fair features in the lantern glow, shadows moving, voices whispering, I could not discern them clearly.

I dared not to intercede. Since then my days are haunted and my prayers remain unanswered.

It was some days before I learned that the Earl himself was responsible for her abduction. What manner of evil drives a man to perform such wickedness? How tragic was her plight, to be shunned, when he learned she was expecting his child. He rejected her, a poor peasant girl, with a few paltry coins and banished her, I learned, much later, to Grampton Village thirty miles south of here.

How helpless and angry I felt; it seemed that the Holy Spirit had deserted me. Although I believe that a man shall love thy enemy, I could find no compassion for the Earl and what he had done. My heart was filled with hatred; it was then I embarked upon my folly.

Prayers and masses for the dead remain unpaid and I made it my business to humbly plead to the Earl upon this matter. But as I stood waiting in his hallway, I regarded the dagger. What was this mystical pagan artefact whose power was said to be beyond comprehension? Was it truly taken into battle against the Vikings by the ancestral Earl of Morchester?

It should have been easy for me to conceal it beneath my robe, to calmly leave the way I came without suspicion or fear that I might get caught. Alas I do not have a thief's guile and my hands were a tremble as I passed through the West Arch. I tripped on a flagstone and the blade clattered to the ground. The noise obviously had disturbed the guards and as they approached I quickly turned out the contents of my purse. I scrambled on the flagstones to catch the rolling coins, my garments spread out around me, concealing the blade beneath. The two guards passed me mocking my apparent clumsiness.

It had been my intention to besmirch the Earl's reputation by spreading the lie that he had brutally murdered Mary with the dagger. He had then buried her and hidden the blade and no evidence could ever be found.

My reckless plan could never have worked. The peasants held the Earl in fearful dread and dared not speak a word against him. I was no gossip monger and I had no stomach to spread such a grisly rumour.

I was desolated to hear that Mary had died in child birth and had been buried in an unmarked grave at Grampton Village. My jealously had achieved nothing but sorrow and no one seemed to care about Mary.

The Earl's humour has changed: he is no longer a man of patience and virtue but sends his men to terrorise the poor folk. How many more innocents must suffer in his search for his missing blade, before my turn comes?

I stole the blade to punish the Earl but already its power works against me. Even in God's House I have no sanctuary and the blade has no place here. I dare not return it for I surely would be found out.

Father forgive me, in my grief and my shame I have resolved to bury the blade with Mary. It is right that I do this for it is the Earl's power that holds her in her grave. If he should ever discover the blade he will have to face what he has done.

Mother Knows Best **

You could have heard Mother's voice three streets away.

"Anthony! How many times do I have to tell you? The dinner's nearly ready. It's not too much trouble to ask you to lay the table now, is it?"

I'd forgotten about that. That's punishable by hanging in our household, you know.

"About time too! Where's your father? He knows what time we serve dinner in this house," her voiced droned on.

There was hell to pay when Dad got home. As I stood on the landing, I heard some language you wouldn't expect to hear from two church going people.

There was worse to come: Mother had found out about Linda. I came downstairs to face the music.

"Anthony, who was that young woman Mrs Hayward saw you with on Friday evening?" Mother was fishing again.

"What young woman, Mother?" I replied, knowing full well whom she meant. "Oh! That's Bill's girlfriend," I said, trying to sound convincing.

"What kind of fool do you take me for?" she stormed. "Don't you dare try to deny it! You've brought shame on the whole family! I don't know

129

how I'll ever be able to show my face in church again."

Poor Mother, she takes everything to heart. I'd been meaning to tell her for some time but I just hadn't got round to it. Of course, Dad didn't help by saying that he already knew about Linda. Mind you he doesn't know the half of it; but then neither did I before meeting Linda! Mother will never understand that it is not just a physical thing. Linda and I love each other and that's what really matters, isn't it?

I agreed to go shopping with Mother the following evening. The trouble was it meant letting Linda down.

"What's the matter, Tony?" asked Linda. "Why do you keep looking at that clock - don't you like this pub or something? Is it your mother again?"

I nodded: "Yeah! She found out about us last night and so to keep the peace I've agreed to go shopping with her this evening."

She leant forward and looked deeply into my eyes: "It's all right I understand, Tony." She kissed me tenderly. "What time have you got to meet her?"

"I said I'd meet her at seven-thirty in the supermarket." I reached out for her hand. "Is that all right, I'm sorry it's messed up our evening. I'll take you somewhere nice tomorrow to make up for it and no excuses."

Time was running out and I rushed headlong through the shopping mall. When I got to the supermarket Mother was nowhere to be seen. Then, to my annoyance, as I looked down the line of checkouts, I saw her packing the shopping. I tried to help her put it away but she made it perfectly clear she didn't require my assistance.

"Where've you been?" she said sharply.

Glancing at the clock I realised to my astonishment that I was on time.

"It's only half-past seven now." I called out angrily. "You must have got here early!" But Mother was already on her way out of the supermarket.

"Thanks a million, Mother!" I muttered. "You've ruined my evening, but you won't stop me going out with Linda."

A couple of days later, I was on my way home after a great evening round at Linda's place. I got to our back door and heard my parents arguing. I paused to listen.

"How do you expect me to feel when my own son doesn't even trust me?" wailed Mother.

"Why should he, when all you do is dominate and dictate to him all the time?" Dad calmly replied.

"That's not true!" she shouted. "I've simply tried to ensure he doesn't get involved with unsuitable people."

"You pompous snob!" said Dad.

"How dare you!" exclaimed Mother.

Dad was having none of this. "It's time you accepted that he's old enough and big enough to look after himself. He's no need to involve you in his private affairs."

"I'm still his mother!" she said defiantly.

"And I'll tell you something else," Dad warned, "if you continue to interfere in his private life you'll end up losing him once and for all."

"We'll see about that!" roared Mother.

There was an uneasy silence. I was surprised and encouraged that Dad had stood up for me like that but I was worried about what Mother would do next. So, I crept back down the side of the house and returned, stamping firmly on the paving so they'd hear me coming. When I got inside you wouldn't have known there'd even been an argument.

To my utter amazement, Mother looked me straight in the eye and said: "Why don't you invite Linda round for tea? How about Thursday evening?"

"So why does she want you to come round for tea?" I asked Linda.

"Be fair, Tony, she's making an effort," Linda suggested.

"Come on, she's up to something!" I persisted.

"She's not up to anything. I suspect your Dad's had a hand in this and she's finally accepted that we're together," said Linda.

"So you're coming round to tea on Thursday night, then?" I asked.

132

"I'm coming all right - I wouldn't miss it for the world," replied Linda.

Mother was surprisingly charming to start with, but she soon swamped Linda with her suffocating politeness. That was just the start of it. The atmosphere became tense when Mother served Linda roast beef. I couldn't believe Mother could be so insensitive when I'd specifically told her Linda was a vegetarian.

"As you two seem to be getting on so well do I hear the sound of wedding bells?" Mother enquired, with all the subtlety of flying brick.

Dad didn't know where to put his face and Linda and I just looked at each other in embarrassment. I tried to change the subject but there's no stopping Mother when she's got the bit between her teeth.

"I do hope you'll get married in Church, only you're not properly married if you don't get married in a church. I am sure you agree Linda, don't you?" challenged Mother.

Linda just made an excuse to go and powder her nose. Whilst she was out of the room Mother wasted no time in telling me exactly what she thought of her.

"And furthermore", Mother warned. "If you continue seeing that girl you needn't think you're staying in this house!"

"Okay, if that's the way you want it, I'll move out tonight!" I yelled defiantly.

Suddenly, Mother fell back in her chair, eyes rolling.

"Oh! No!" I thought. "Mother's having one of her turns again".

Turning white and gasping for breath, she spluttered: "It's all your fault, Anthony, you've done this to me."

I dashed to the kitchen and fetched a glass of water with her pills. Her shaking hands snatched them from me.

"Are you feeling better, now?" I asked presently. "I'll talk to Linda, Okay Mother?"

Mother never answered.

"You're making things very difficult for me. Don't ask me to choose between the two of you."

"Do what you like!" she stormed.

I drove Linda home in silence which was broken only by the sound of the windscreen wipers beating against the torrential rain. I wanted to tell Linda how I really felt but the words would not come out. I wanted to apologise for the way the evening had gone but Mother's words drowned out my thoughts.

"Get rid of her, she's no good for you," Mother had warned.

Those words kept ringing in my ears. They grew louder and louder. Suddenly I couldn't stand it any longer.

"No!" I shouted, as I pulled off the main road and into a lay–by. My knuckles were white as I gripped the steering wheel, my hands shaking with rage. "No! She's not getting her way this time. Dad's right, those bad turns are all an act; she has no right to interfere with my life. Why didn't Dad back me up when I needed him?"

"Look, Tony" said Linda calmly, "it's up to you to stand up to her. Don't blame your Dad, he deals with her in his own way."

"I did stand up to her," I protested, "but you don't know my mother."

"Oh, I think I know her well enough," Linda said. She looked at me in a way I'd never seen before. "I heard it all from the bathroom. I heard what she said. She thinks she's won doesn't she? But she hasn't! And we're going to wipe that smirk right off her face, aren't we Tony?" A look of triumph flickered in her eyes.

Looking at Linda I realised that here was someone who was more than a match for my mother. Something told me that from this day on I was free of my mother forever. Then I found out why.

Linda smiled. A grim smile.

"Tell your mother, I'm pregnant!"

Mrs Philpot

Elizabeth Philpot, a young widow, had secured a position with a local building firm as a part time typist. Things had been very difficult for her bringing up her daughter, Maureen, single handed but her new found earnings would help pay for those little extras.

On her first day she was asked to do some typing for John Perkins. Although he held a senior position with the company she thought it odd that he should ask her so many personal questions. She reasoned that he was just taking a friendly interest as she was a new member of staff.

"May I have the pleasure of giving you a lift home?" Perkins grinned, his teeth sparkled like in a tooth a paste advert. "you don't have a car, do you?"

"I have to leave at three to pick my daughter up from school."

"Ah yes, I was forgetting, you're part time, aren't you?"

Elizabeth nodded. She'd felt embarrassed, almost ashamed. Perkins had that effect on people.

He continued to probe her with questions. She was very uneasy about him but she dared not complain to his boss. After all, he held a senior position, she didn't want to risk losing her job.

"I'm leaving the office early," he causally announced one day, "so I'll give you a lift."

She gulped. Her mind raced for a tactful reply.

"Thanks all the same, I wouldn't want to put you to any trouble. Besides, I've got to pick my daughter up from school."

His reply shot back in a split second. He wouldn't be put off that easily.

"Oh, it's no trouble at all. I can easily make a diversion to the school. No trouble at all."

Perhaps her imagination was getting the better of her but she sensed that his devious eyes were scrutinizing her body and that in his minds-eye he had reached her underwear and probably further.

She took a deep breath. Quickly, she'd made her way towards the door.

"No really, I'd rather not."

He grabbed her arm. He pulled her towards him.

"Oh, but I insist."

The horrors of rape quickly flashed through her mind, they were alone in the office. Luckily she saw a colleague walking down the corridor.

She shouted: "Paul! Glad I caught you."

Perkins had instantly let go of Elizabeth. She grasped the opportunity to be out of range of his tentacles and walked with Paul down the corridor.

The weekend gave her the opportunity to spend more time with Maureen and on Saturday they went shopping. The last thing that Elizabeth had wanted was to be stopped in the street by her interfering neighbour, Mrs Grumps. She made a point of knowing everybody's business, particularly newcomers to the area, so it didn't take long before Mrs Grumps was poking her nose in where it wasn't wanted.

"My, my, how she's grown," Mrs Grumps patted Maureen on the head, "yes, she's coming on a treat. She's looking a little bit peaky though, perhaps she's not getting enough to eat."

Elizabeth bit her tongue: "She never goes hungry, Mrs Grumps."

Mrs Grumps wasn't famous for her tact. She was a master for saying the wrong thing at the wrong time.

"Yes, well, I expect you do your best given the circumstances. I always say a child needs a father."

"She won't get one whilst I'm standing around talking to you. Good day, Mrs Grumps."

Holding Maureen's hand tightly, Elizabeth stormed off leaving Mrs Grumps speechless. Elizabeth was feeling very pleased with herself for putting Mrs Grumps in her place but at the same time she was very angry. The implication that she was a single parent through choice wasn't justified; her husband had been killed in an accident. Anyway, it was none of Mrs Grumps business.

Sunday was a lovely morning when Elizabeth took Maureen to the park. Maureen loved that. She was in her element feeding the ducks and watching the birds fly overhead. As she hopped and skipped,

138

she was greeted by a beautiful white swan whom had taken a shine to her packet of sweets.

"Can I give him one, Mummy?"

"I don't know if he'll eat them, but drop one on the ground for him. No, don't feed it to him, he might bite."

The swan swallowed the sweet whole. Maureen laughed.

"Look, Mummy, he's ate it all up."

"Yes, he's a greedy Mr Swan, isn't he?"

The swan flapped his wings, his webbed feet took a few hobbled steps and he leapt into the water, graciously gliding down stream. Elizabeth and Maureen walked along the lake's bank and the sun began to raise its heat. Maureen noticed the ice cream van.

"Mummy, can I have an ice cream."

"Yes all right, Maureen, I did promise you one, didn't I."

"Please, allow me to get them," a voice echoed.

Elizabeth turned round: "Oh, it's you, Mr Perkins, what a surprise!"

"Is this your daughter? She looks just like you. Hello, Maureen."

"What's your name?" Maureen asked Perkins.

"Say hello to Mr Perkins, Maureen. Mummy does some work for Mr Perkins."

Maureen looked up at him. She was very shy. so she stood close to her mother and held her hand tightly.

"What flavour ice cream would she like?"

"No really, I couldn't expect you to. Thank you all the same, Mr Perkins."

"Oh no need to be so formal, Elizabeth. Please call me John," he replied with a sickly smile, "two cornets be all right?"

"No, I couldn't possibly..."

"Nonsense. I insist."

He'd joined the ice cream van's queue despite Elizabeth's protests. She hesitated for a moment before marching Maureen out of the park with the echo of her daughter's screaming tears trailing behind.

Elizabeth had dreaded going to work the next day for the prospect of facing Perkins wasn't something to look forward to. She pondered whether she should have been gracious enough to have accepted the ice creams. On the other hand, in doing so, she would have encouraged him and she hadn't wanted that to happen. Telling him straight, to leave her alone, was the only answer.

She made her way to the office after taking Maureen to school. As she walked, she became conscious of footsteps coming towards her. Glancing over her shoulder she could see Perkins behind her. She started to walk faster but the footsteps drew nearer. There was nobody else in sight and she began to panic as Perkins was almost upon her. Suddenly his hand gripped her shoulder. She screamed hysterically.

"Elizabeth, control yourself, what is the matter with you?"

Tears rolled down her cheeks as she continued to scream. Her hysterics had taken him by surprise. This would do nothing for his reputation but he was sure nobody had seen or heard anything. He fled. She ran home. Sobbing, she'd phoned in sick.

Somehow she'd plucked up the courage to go to work the following day but fortunately Perkins was in a meeting all morning. It was then she'd decided to tell her colleague, Mary, about the incident.

"Oh don't worry about it, love, all the girls have had their turn with him. Perky the Creepy Crawly, we call him."

"But how do I get rid of him? I can't stand him. Honestly, Mary, I'm desperate. I can't go on like this. I'll have to leave if it comes to it."

"Look just sit down and have a nice cup of tea. There's one easy way to get rid of him."

"How? How can I do that?"

"You have to play him at his own game. When Perky next asks you out. Say yes!"

"What to that creep? Come on, Mary, you must be joking?"

"Just trust me. I promise you, it's the only way. He'll probably take you out to dinner. He usually goes to the Lobster Pot. He shows his company card and gets a big discount. The cheapskate. Then he'll invite you back to his place. For a cup of coffee he'll say. It's obvious what he's got in mind."

"Wait a minute! The thought of having dinner with him is bad enough, but there's no way I'm going to bed with him."

Mary laughed: "Of course you won't, silly. Once he's got you in his flat, he'll slip off to the bathroom." Mary giggled. "Gawd knows what he does in there. Whilst he's powdering his nose or whatever he does, me and a couple of the girls will slip into the flat and surprise him! Easy-Peasy!"

"Oh I don't know, what if something was to go wrong?"

"Oh relax, nothing will go wrong, he wouldn't know what to do anyway!"

Against her better judgement, Elizabeth had decided to go along with Mary's scheme. When she'd thought about it, what other options were there?

As Mary predicted, Perkins took Elizabeth to the Lobster Pot and produced his company card to the head waiter. He needn't have bothered, the waiter knew him well enough. He wined and dined her, talked about himself, his ambitions, his dreams. Predictably, he'd asked Elizabeth to go back to his place for coffee. She'd agreed. She'd come this far, there was no turning back.

She sat on his couch. He looked at her, producing another one of his sickly smiles, then played his next card.

"Oh do excuse me, Elizabeth. Make yourself comfortable, I'll be back in a jiffy."

He went into the bathroom. Elizabeth was very nervous. Her eyes gazed around his flat. She became aware of the sadness in it. Everything seemed cold, unwanted, lonely. It was as if he kept his real personality locked away in that flat. Jekyll went to the office and left Hyde at home. For the first time she'd felt sorry for him. In his bumbling way, perhaps all he was trying to do was to find love, a companion, a friend. He was a sad, pathetic, lonely man but she and her friends had schemed to humiliate him.

She'd decided to leave. She'd crept to the door and opened it. Perkins had returned from the bathroom wearing only his dressing gown.

"Was there somebody at the door, Elizabeth?"

"Err, no, it's a little warm in here. Just getting some air, John."

"Just thought I'd slip into something a little more comfortable," he continued. "Relax. Enjoy!" he whispered.

"Oh my God," she thought to herself, "how corny." She tried to change the subject. "You were going to show me your holiday snaps?"

"Never mind those. I'm in the mood for love."

He took off his gown and stood before her naked. Although she was shocked to see him standing there with nothing on, surprisingly she wasn't frightened. She just couldn't help thinking what an awful sight he looked.

Mary and two other girls burst into the room. They took a succession of photographs of the naked and surprised Perkins. They then whisked Elizabeth out of the flat and into the getaway car. They laughed and giggled, but Elizabeth knew she'd done the wrong thing.

Yet nothing could have prepared Elizabeth for the shock she received the following morning. It took several days for her to take in what the news broadcaster had read on local radio.

"Last night a man died after jumping out of the window from his top floor flat. He has been named as John Perkins. The dead man lived and worked in the area. "

She never returned to her job. She would have probably suffered a nervous breakdown had it not been for her daughter. Three months after the tragedy she was offered another job a hundred miles away. It was a chance to start a fresh.

John Perkins had left a suicide note. He was a lonely man. All he wanted was to love someone and care for them. He thought Elizabeth was the girl of his dreams. But she'd betrayed him, just like the others.

Elizabeth and Maureen got into a taxi which would take them to the station to catch the train to their new life. The removal van would make its own way. Mrs Grumps watched them leave. She couldn't resist one last dig.

"I'm not sorry to see her go," she told a neighbour. "Disgusting wild parties. These single parents are all the same. Shameful. Her boyfriend, you know, killed himself. On drugs he was. And her, if the truth be known. Good riddance, that's what I say."

My Last Escape *

At last I'd managed to escape because this time I'd planned it more thoughtfully. There was only one thing stopping me crossing the border - Officer Lean.

I was shaking with fear. I held my breath until I felt my lungs would burst. Sweat matted the hair on the back of my neck and my scalp prickled as I watched him through a clearing in the bushes.

How could he have know I'd come this way? I grasped the wooden crucifix around my neck and prayed as I'd never done before. But Lean drew closer and closer - it was only matter of time.

Suddenly two men appeared out of nowhere and set upon the startled Lean. If he'd heard my gasp of surprise it surely would have given the game away. The bandits had knocked him to the ground and were beating him mercilessly. He reached for his gun but it was kicked away in the struggle. If I hadn't intervened he would have received a fatal blow at any moment.

Who would have thought that those brutal beatings in the ring, from my Campus days, would help me to save a man's life. Although I say it myself, I was too quick for them, they ran away like a couple of scared rabbits. As the dust settled, Lean stood in front of me, pointing his gun at my head.

Why did I help a man who only wanted to kill me? I can't claim that God had told me to do it. I didn't do it to try and win Lean's favour - as if my show of bravado would influence him anyway! I just knew I had to help - I would have done the same for anyone in that position.

Though God is my witness, Lean was the law. He'd hunted me all the way to the border and he meant to take me back to prison. Business was business. If I tried to make a break for it he'd sooner shoot me dead than run after me.

Without explanation, he suddenly ordered me to head back towards the checkpoint. Getting passed the guards was child's play for Lean. He told one of them that he was under orders to take me over the border. The guard was suspicious but Lean barked him into submission.

I can barely find words to describe the elation I felt as I crossed the border to freedom. I fell to my knees to thank God for watching over me. I turned to express my gratitude, but Lean had gone. He would have to return to the prison to face his superiors and be branded a failure. I was now a free man. How much greater was his sacrifice for me?

The Mystery Woman

It seemed like an ordinary day when I set off in my car to go shopping at my favourite seaside town. The weather was cold but bright; it made a change from all the rain we'd been having. Everything was normal as I drove along the country lane that led me to the town. I like to park on the sea front; firstly, there is no charge, secondly, I enjoy a stroll along the promenade.

When I arrived at the sea front I prepared to reverse into a parking space. To my annoyance, another car shot in the space before me. I tooted my horn in frustration but the woman simply got out of her car and, with a toss of her pony tail, strode off in the direction of the town.

As I continued my search for a parking space I almost met with an accident at a junction. As I turned left I was forced to slam on my brakes to avoid a woman motorist who had pulled out in front of me.

"What on earth do you think you're doing?" I called out.

I wound down my window to give her a piece of my mind but I was struck dumb. It was the same woman who had only just pinched my car parking space. Who was this woman? How did she get there? I couldn't understand it.

Feeling a little shaken I continued my journey. I observed the woman, in my rear view mirror, heading in the other direction.

As it was a nice day I decided to go for a walk along the cliffs. From this vantage point I could watch the steam train running alongside the golf course. When I got there I was amazed to see, yet again, this woman walking towards me. I knew it was her. She was middle aged, had a very distinctive hooked nose, her hair was long and tied back in a neat pony tail. She was wearing a grey coat and long black boots.

As we drew nearer she seemed to make a deliberate move to avoid my path. Perhaps she was embarrassed over the two motor incidents I concluded. I was still a little shaken up over the near miss myself and was disappointed that I hadn't had the chance to apologies.

After a while I decided to turn back and make my way along the sea front. The waves crashed against the rocks below sending up an invigorating spray. What a wonderful place the seaside is: so much more tranquil than the hurly-burly of the high season.

Presently I arrived at the edge of the town. I saw the mysterious woman standing on the opposite side of the road and I called out to her. I'm sure she saw me but she slipped away into a tea room. My imagination began to work over time. Perhaps she was some kind of spy?

I decided to venture in for a cup of coffee. I wondered whether I was just tired or were my eyes just playing tricks on me. I purchased my drink and sat down near the doorway. I closed my eyes and sipped my hot refreshment. I would have probably dosed off if it hadn't been for the sound of the door chiming when another customer came in.

I was snapped out of my reverie. I wondered where I was for a moment but then I saw her across the tea room. She sat, by the curtains, sipping her tea and eating a hot buttered tea cake. I plucked up the courage to accost her.

"Excuse me," I said approaching her, "I just wanted to take this opportunity to apologies for my rudeness earlier."

She looked at me as if she didn't have the faintest idea what I was talking about. I felt confused and embarrassed but before I had time to make amends, she gathered her things together and left the tea room.

As I finished my coffee I couldn't help feeling hurt that she had snubbed me. Surely she must have heard me shout at her, I only wanted to apologies. Perhaps she felt I was a little too forward and was about to make an improper suggestion. I felt sickened by the thought that she would consider me some sort of pervert. I couldn't let the matter lie. I had to speak to her urgently but I had no idea which way she went.

I left the tea room and I must admit I was perspiring quite heavily. The cool breeze from the sea was welcoming as I made my way up the hill towards the local theatre. I enquired at the box office as to the availability of a ticket for the evening performance.

"Yes sir, you're lucky, we were booked-up tonight but we've just had a cancellation. Those two ladies have just brought the ticket back."

I looked across the foyer which was decorated with photographs of past productions of the resident company and saw the two ladies studying them. As they turned round I stared in amazement. I realised how close I'd come to making a fool of myself earlier. How upset I'd become in the tea room over a woman I didn't even know. Standing before me was the mystery woman I had encountered earlier and her sister. But who was who? They were identical twins!

Newborn

That certainly feels better. I'm all fresh and clean now that the nurse has washed all that mess off me. What's the weather like outside at the moment? Hum, doesn't look too bad. It's been pretty boring stuck inside these past months I can tell you.

Watch out! Where's the nurse taking me now? I should have guessed, it's time to meet the family. No prizes for guessing that the bald headed man with a silly grin on his face is Grandad. Yep. No doubt about it. The old dear standing next to him, crying her eyes out, "isn't he lovely!" must be Grandma. Here we go, the nurse has passed me over to Granny. Hope she stops crying, or I'll drown in two minutes flat.

"Hey Grandma! Yes you, funny face! This is not a funeral you know."

What the heck's she saying to me? 'Koochy-koo!" What in heaven's name does that mean? What strange dialect is that supposed to be?

"Have a heart, Granny, you can't expect someone of my age to learn foreign languages, can you?"

Hold-up! Who's got hold of me now? Oh no. Don't say that's my Dad! He looks a right drip! Mum must be about somewhere. Ah, that must be her. Hey! She's not what I expected. A nice looking lady I can tell you. I could quite fancy her. The question is, what does she see in this drip here? He's got horrible teeth.

Two days later and I'm still in this hospital. Grandad's still grinning, Grandma's still crying, Dad's still looks like a drip. Mum's just fed me so I'm feeling quite satisfied. Listen-up! They are discussing what name they are going to give me. Oh no, please no, not Reginald! Can you imagine being called Reginald? What will the kids at school call me? Reggie? or Reg? No thanks, think of something else, guys. Yeah, that's not bad, well done Mum. You must be joking Dad. I'm not going around with a name like Cuthbert. I'd have to emigrate or something.

I'm at home now, lying in my cot and my birth certificate's on the table. Reginald Cuthbert Brown. Can you believe it? That's my rotten name! Reginald Cuthbert Brown. Oh, well, I wonder what Australia's like? I wonder if other kids like me are lying in their cots surrounded by gigantic toy animals? Now what on earth am I supposed to do with a teddy bear that's twice my size? Here she comes again, Granny, come to rattle those stupid things in my face.

"Leave it out will you, Granny. Where's Mum gone? Tell her I'm hungry."

Now what's she doing? Why is she tapping her fingers on her lips and making silly noises? Wonders will never cease, she's just spoken in English!

153

"Yes, Granny, that's right. Yes, Granny. Yes. For goodness sake, Granny, I'm not deaf. I heard you the first time."

If she says: "who's Grandma's best little boy?' once more, I'll scream. I really will. Oh no, this is torture beyond belief. She singing me a lullaby of all things. I think I prefer looking at Dad's teeth.

Having survived Granny's singing the other week; I'm out for a walk in the park with Mum and Dad. Well, actually, I'm not walking - they are. I'm quietly lying in my pram enjoying the sunshine. It's nice being a baby, 'cause these very attractive women keep coming over to have a peep at me. Now some of these females are wearing very low cut dresses I can tell you.

Now this is quite ridiculous. Here I am just a couple of weeks old and Dad's already planning my future. He's reserved me a place at the St Morris Junior and Infant School, five years this coming September.

"Now just a minute, Dad, just hold your horses. I'm not going to some rotten boy's school when I'm eleven. No way am I doing that, so you can forget it."

Good for Mum, she says I would be better off at a mixed school. Now I'll second that, all those lovely girls, oh yes please!

Thank goodness Dad's shut up. Perhaps Mum and I can get some peace. Cor, I wouldn't mind getting a piece of that. Wow, she is gorgeous, what a beautiful female. I must say I'm enjoying this summer. All the girls walk about in short skirts showing their flesh. Lovely! Can't say I'm looking forward to this winter Dad's always on about. Apparently everybody puts on layers of clothes just to keep warm. That means I won't be able to look at the girl's legs or lust after their shapely figures.

He's off again, Dad is. He's talking about my future once more. He's on about me going to University of all things. For one thing, how does he know I'll have the intelligence to pass all those exams? As it happens I'm sure I'll take after Mum - bright, clever, interesting, attractive. But for all he knows I could turn out just like him - a right dickhead. Sorry to get out of my pram once again but I'm not standing for this.

"Hey, Dad, listen to me for just a minute! There is no way I'm going to follow in your footsteps and be an accountant, so just put that out of your mind straight away."

If he thinks I'm going to waste my life away being stuck in an office all day he's got to be mad. When I grow up I'm going to be someone famous like a pop star or a professional sportsman. Now if I became a pop star I could change my name, couldn't I? How about Elvis Brown, the youngest swinger in town? Hey, I just thought of that, good, eh? Or I could be a tennis player, now there's a thought. Just think, playing mixed doubles at Wimbledon! Sounds good to me!

This sounds serious. Mum and Dad are talking about having another baby.

"Hang about, Mum and Dad, don't I get a say in this? We've only got a two bedroom house you know! I'm not sharing my bedroom with anyone else and that's final. It might snore. I need my beauty sleep. Dad shared a room with two brothers and look what happened to him!"

They're not listening to me. I may as well not be here for all the good it's doing, but I know just the thing to get their attention.

"Mum! My nappy needs changing!"

Once A Pun A Time

Once a pun a time Malcolm Moore sat in his favourite chair, he bit his nails and waited for a cry. It wasn't the cry he was expecting; he'd bitten his finger and he cried out when could so easily have cried in. To say this was a nail bitting situation was to hit the nail on the head only it was his finger. It could be said this was splitting hares but then again not rabbits. Fortunately it wasn't a mega bite as computers hadn't been invented back then but oddly enough windows had been. He was about to become a father for the fourth time but nothing could be father from the truth to say he wanted a girl. He was hoping for a son to help him with the farm; he didn't consider a girl would be just as capable.

His farm was small but prosperous. There were many small farmers like himself who grew crops whilst the hairdressers would cut them. Life was hard, very hard, but he loved it. Malcolm was a yeoman and therefore he grew potatoes.

Malcolm then heard a cry of a baby and his heart was beating like a drum beat of a native tribe. He got his guitar and quickly composed some chords to fit the beat. He preferred chords to denims. All he needed now was a tune but he didn't have one so he settled for a spangle. Malcolm's heart was beating even faster as heard the sound of footsteps getting nearer and nearer. Anxious, he put his head in his lap but when his sister came in she told him to put his head back on.

"It's a boy, you have a son".

"No, but I've got the Daily Mirror" he replied.

Then the penny dropped to coin a phrase and he ran upstairs to his wife and child. He was over the moon at having a son. His house was small but he'd find space for his son.

"Mary, I love you" he said.

"You'll have to wait" she snapped.

Malcolm stuck her together again. Luckily he always carried some glue in his pocket. It was a habit he'd stuck to over the years.

As the years went by Malcolm and Mary had two more sons and life seemed simple and sweet. However a new industrial age had begun with deadly mines, his, hers, yours and theirs. Dangerous conditions existed in the factories and many people lived in an unhealthy environment in ugly polluted towns. Farming methods were improved and wealthy land owners became richer for their efforts. Yet the small farmer like Malcolm, he was five feet nothing, were being forced to sell their land. A movement came about to enclose land and this led to a great increase in the number of large estates at the expense of hatchbacks. Against his better judgement, Malcolm sold his land to three business partners and they were interested in new farming methods. They liked the idea of sowing seeds in rows instead of being scattered all over the field in a willy nilly fashion as †hey didn't like Willy Nilly's fashion. The idea of using horses to plough the fields was put forward but results of a gallop poll indicated horses didn't make good farmers and were a bit of a nightmare. So they hoofed this suggestion into touch although they didn't play Rugby. Tractors were also rejected because of the price of petrol owing to trouble in the middle east which they believed was on the Norfolk and Lincolnshire border. The partners though realised it was important not to waste useful land so rotation crops were started. This meant hairdressers were cutting crops much more frequently and so the skin head craze began to emerge in a big way. Malcolm and his family were able to live for free or four in one of the partner's houses on condition they moved into the town. Malcolm wasn't keen on this although he could watch the match on a Saturday. Mary didn't see the appeal of watching a match and their only use, as far as she was concerned, was for lighting a fire.

So the Moores moved to the town unwillingly. Unwillingly was a town near Bradford and when they arrived they were shocked to see skinheads everywhere who'd moved to the town to be nearer the hairdressers. A skinhead approached Malcolm picking his nose. He'd a choice of noses and he'd settled on a large one. At the time Malcolm was standing in some dirt which represented a road as the road didn't want to come that day. Malcolm didn't like the skinhead's haircut and he told him so.

"So this is what the Industrial Revolution has given us" moaned Malcolm.

"Na, mate," replied the skinhead. "It's the Crop Revolution."

"You look like a hedgehog," laughed Malcolm.

The skinhead wasn't amused. Malcolm wasn't the most tactful of people and was for ever upsetting people. He'd previously put his foot in it with the chiropodist and his dentist had his fill of him when Malcolm kept mouthing off on how easy his job was. The patient/health professional relationship decayed rapidly from then on. For whatever reason Malcolm was reluctant to volunteer if he'd any problems with his teeth and his dentist would have to extract the information from him. Malcolm had to concede though a dentist was the sort of job someone could get their teeth into and the routine was appealing especially with all the drills. He also enjoyed the trip to the dentist practice as it involved using the canal which was a very pleasant route. Right now, Malcolm had an offended skinhead to deal with who threw his fist at Malcolm. Malcolm ducked and the skinhead had to retrieve his limb which had landed in a privet. Malcolm tried to cool matters by claiming he'd meant no 'arm but the skinhead now had the opportunity to hedge his bets. Fortunately for Malcolm he decided not pursue the matter any further and went off to the hairdressers.

Mary wasn't too keen on the vast amount of smoke in the town and she soon learned the potteries were a significant feature of the town, so much so, pot smoking was an every day occurrence. Malcolm made no comment about this, he was preoccupied chewing bubble gum. Mary didn't like him chewing this stuff but Malcolm reasoned a man's gotta chew what a man's gotta chew.

Malcolm then noticed a game of cricket was taking place in a field opposite and went to watch. He could have gone to clock but he chose to go to watch. There were two batmen on the field, one the real thing and the other an impersonator. Robin was watching from the pavilion and kept repeating "Holly Jimmy Cricket." The bowler bowled the first ball and followed immediately with a second and a third and the batsman complained it was unfair to expect him to hit three balls all at once. The umpire agreed and declared a "no ball." The bowler protested stating he couldn't possibly bowl without a ball. The umpire was initially stumped by this remark but then he creased up laughing. The rest of the cricketers couldn't give a toss and just wanted to get on with the game. One of the cricketers kept going off to the pavilion toilets with the runs which made him feel so unwell it knocked him for six and he ended up being sick on all fours.

Malcolm and Mary had a serious chat and decided this wasn't the life for them and approached the partners about buying their old farm back.

Fortunately the partners had lost interest in farming and were only too glad to get their money back. Malcolm and his family moved back to the farm where they lived and worked for the rest of their lives. They didn't miss the town and neither did they madam it.

One Hell Of A Day

"Yes, hello. Can I speak to Bob, please? Tell him it's his wife, Pauline."

The very busy assistant was caught on the hop. She nearly didn't answer the phone but thought she'd better in case it was something important. She'd a hundred and one things to do and no time to do them in.

"Bob who?"

"There's only one Bob, isn't there? Surely you know Bob? Bob Graham. Ring any bells?"

"Yes, I'm sorry. Of course, Bob!"

"Bingo!"

Pauline's sarcasm had turned the assistant's face bright pink. Pauline was very impatient.

"Well, can I speak to him, please?"

"He's not available at the moment, can I get him to call you?"

Pauline exploded louder than an atom bomb. If the assistant didn't get her husband to the phone that instant she wouldn't be responsible for her actions. The poor assistant, her face didn't know what to do.

It was all Bob's fault. At least that's what Pauline said. He'd let her oversleep that morning. Why didn't he wake her? And because of him she was having one hell of a day.

First the kitchen tap had sprung a leak and Bob had gone off with the cheque book so she couldn't pay the plumber. The milkman hadn't turned up so the children had to go without their cornflakes and Amy always sulked when she couldn't have her usual breakfast.   As for Darren, he'd been his usual annoying self. Apart from playing a handful of practical jokes, which she'd become accustomed to, he'd decided he'd got tummy ache and was not well enough to go to school. Of course, nothing to do with the fact that he hadn't done his Maths homework and Mr Beckett would be less than pleased.

Blow and if that wasn't enough, the postman delivered a letter from the *friendly* electricity company threatening to disconnect the supply unless they pay up within seven days.

What else could be wrong? Everything! The assistant was learning all about it.

"Give me one good reason why I can't speak to Bob?"

"The curtain's gone up, that's why."

"Look, I'm not interested in his curtains. I demand to speak to my husband." ¹

"I'm sorry Mrs Graham, It's just not possible for you to speak to your husband at the moment, you must realise that. Now if you would leave me your number I'll get him to ring you later."

"He knows the number, stupid. At least he should do, we've had the same one for fifteen years. Now I'm running out patience. I demand to speak to my husband!"

164

Pauline just wouldn't listen. She'd had it up to here. It was imperative she spoke to her husband immediately.

It wasn't fair of Bob to leave everything to her all the time. It wasn't him who had to do the housework, get the children to and from school, cook, pay the milkman or get the dustbin bags ready for the Refuge Collectors. Explain to the telephone canvassers that she was happy with what she'd got thank you very much. In any case, they couldn't possibly afford double glazing on Bob's pitiful salary.

Annoyingly, Bob didn't have to deal with any of that. How could he? He was hardly ever at home.

The children saw very little of him. Sunday was about their only chance, but he spent most of that catching up on his *beauty* sleep. His snoring was so loud it could drown the noise of the Rolling Stones playing full volume at a Rock Concert. If that wasn't unpleasant enough he would round off the unwanted entertainment with frequent breaks of wind. This was a ritual that Pauline had come to detest.

Eventually he would surface around lunch time, stagger downstairs in his crumpled pyjamas and sit at the dining table, waiting to be fed. Sometimes he would muster up the energy to lift the newspaper off the table and bury his head in the sports pages. Normally his nose ventured no further save for a quick snoop at page three - his eyes would never entertain *intellectual* news. Not until lunch was over would he contemplate getting dressed. Even then, he'd usually lie down on the sofa and repeat his ritual.

Pauline had had enough. Bob was to come to the phone that instant.

"Tell you what I can do, Mrs Graham. When the break comes I'll see if Bob can speak to you."

"Tea break I suppose! I was under the impression that he didn't have one? At least that's what he told me!"

"I don't understand you, Mrs Graham. There's always an interval after act one."

"Act one? What are you talking about?"

"Act one for Richard, of course."

"Who's Richard?"

"Richard The Third. Didn't he tell you? It's the matinee performance."

"What is? Can you run that by me again?"

The assistant sighed. She'd better things to do. Mrs Graham was winding her up, surely? She explained that Pauline's husband, Bob Graham the actor, was on stage in a production of Richard The Third. Didn't Pauline know that? Hadn't she already told Pauline that the curtain had gone up?

"Now just a minute Miss, whatever your name is. My husband isn't an actor. He works for R.S.C. Limited. He's the manager in the Soft Furnishings Department."

"In that case, Mrs Graham, we're talking about different Bob Grahams. This is The Royal Shakespeare Company and the Bob Graham that I know is most definitely an actor. I'm sure he doesn't know the first thing about soft furnishings."

For the first time Mrs Graham was lost for words. Eventually she muttered a feeble apology and quickly replaced the receiver.

"Darren!"

"What, Mum?"

"When I asked you to phone your father at work, I expected you to ring R.S.C. Limited. Not William Shakespeare!"

Playing the innocent was pointless. He'd had his practical joke. The inevitable smack immediately followed. Darren yelled. It was one hell of a day.

The Priceless Book

"Mr Reynolds. It is my privilege and pleasure to inform you that this is indeed a rare and valuable book." Watkins, an educated and a well spoken antique dealer, thirstily licked his lips in anticipation, "I am most pleased to offer you five thousand pounds."

Without even waiting for an answer Watkins withdrew his cheque book from his tweed jacket pocket and clicked his ball pen into writing mode. It was purely a matter of routine for him.

"To whom shall I make the cheque payable?"

Reynolds didn't answer. He sat back in his old dilapidated armchair, lit his pipe and quietly puffed it as the smoke gently formed circular rings before his eyes. Watkins waited patiently. He waited for what must have seemed an eternity. He then realised that Reynolds had no intention of answering his question.

"Mr Reynolds? Is there something you want to ask me? Is there something I have failed to explain? You do understand what I am offering you?" His patronising manner was everything he intended it to be. "I am offering you five thousand pounds for your book. It is a great deal of money, I am sure you agree?"

Reynolds looked at him for a brief moment before he rose from his armchair and placed the book under the broken leg of his dining table. He returned to his armchair and continued smoking his pipe.

"Marvellous old book that," Reynolds muttered presently displaying a riled grin, "exactly the right width. Three inches and three-sixteenths. Not found another book to replace it not that I'd want to anyway. It's been in the family for over a hundred years. Dining table's all wobbly without that book."

Watkins chuckled nervously: "You will be able to buy yourself a brand new table with all the money."

Reynolds shook his head. He was appalled at the thought of some tasteless piece of modern furniture cluttering up precious space in his cottage.

"Don't want no modern rubbish. Solid oak that is. Don't make 'em like that any more."

Watkins wiped the sweat from his forehead, his bushy eyebrows stood out like some over grown privet hedge. His trade was going through a very bad patch and the bank manager was running out of patience. The bank would foreclose on his business if things didn't improve within the next few months. They were in no mood to take the risk of investing capital into a Company that was lacking a healthy bank balance. It was precisely for that reason he wanted a loan or his overdraft extended. How could he expand otherwise?

Watkins desperately needed that book. He knew it would fetch, at an auction, at least ten times what he was offering Reynolds, even in its dusty and worn condition.

"Mr Reynolds, let us not beat about the bush. I will pay you ten thousand pounds for the book and I will let you have any antique dining table that I have available in my shop. Just think, Mr Reynolds, ten grand and a free table. What do you say?"

Reynolds was unmoved. He explained to Watkins that the money was of no consequence to him. What would he do with it? He was happy and contented living in his cottage. His pension was just enough to live on, he needed nothing else. If he suddenly came into money he would be invaded by friends, acquaintances and distant relatives he never knew he had. Everyone would be out to bleed him dry of his new found wealth. The tranquillity he'd come to enjoy in his cottage would be lost forever.

Watkins's desperation slipped into fifth gear. He'd been too patient for too long.

"Mr Reynolds. What you have there, supporting the broken leg of your old oak dining table, is one the finest and rarest books of Victorian England. It is reputed that Royalty once owned a copy. I have knowledge of only four copies in the entire World. Yours is now the fifth."

"Wasn't very popular then, was it, this book? Doesn't say much for its author if only handful of copies were printed. Mind you, I'm not surprised, I soon got bored reading it."

Watkins was offended. Judging by his reaction anyone would have thought he'd written it himself.

"It contains some of the finest poetry ever written!" he stormed.

Reynolds laughed: "Poetry! Huh! Some of it doesn't even rhyme!"

Watkins was speechless for a few moments. He realised that he'd obviously underestimated Reynolds. He'd taken him for some silly old man and an easy push over. But this old boy was no fool. This was his way of bargaining for a higher price. Watkins knew he would have to make him a more realistic offer.

"My partner is going to kill me for this, Mr Reynolds, but what the hell, I must have that book. Fifteen thousand pounds, Mr Reynolds, I'm offering you fifteen thousand and that's my final offer."

Reynolds never flinched. He wondered slowly into the kitchen and put the kettle on.

"Tea?" he called out.

Twenty-thousand pounds!"

Reynolds nonchalantly returned from the kitchen. He withdrew his pipe from his mouth.

"Cash?"

Watkins nodded submissively, opened his brief case and counted out twenty-thousand pounds in used notes. Reynolds knew he had the cash. His type always did. Reynolds removed the book from under the table leg and handed it to him. Watkins carefully placed it in his briefcase and left.

171

Watkins was a typical dealer out to make a quick profit. If he'd bothered to have researched the book's history properly, he would have known that there were several fake copies in existence. These fakes looked so authentic they were almost perfect. Reynolds could tell the difference, Watkins obviously could not.

Reynolds placed another book under the table leg and glanced up at his grandfather clock that had ticked so reliably for many years. He would have twenty minutes rest before it was time to meet his next customer.

The Red Door *

Beaven House had all the faded elegance of Victorian Gothic, always destined to be a home for the elderly. It didn't worry Sam because he remembered playing there as a boy.

He was shown to his room complete with en-suite bathroom and emergency alarm system - should he ever need it. Deidre had encouraged him to go there as he was getting a bit of a handful now. Sam smiled. If only she knew how much of a handful she was when she was young. A chip off the old block you might say.

Whilst waiting for supper, his mind wandered back to the days when he used to sneak into the walled garden with his little friend, Emily. There was an abundance of flowers, with a luscious green sward dotted with mature trees.

Perhaps because they were forbidden to go there, it made it seem all the more wonderful. He could only remember one incident when they were apprehended by Harold the gardener.

"Come on young, Sam," barked Harold. His silver hair and grey moustache gave him a superior air. "Mr Forrester doesn't want you playing out here. Don't let me catch you in here ever again," he warned.

Sam retreated to the side gate where Emily was waiting for him. They peeped round to see Harold disappearing into Beaven House through a red door at the side.

"Is that his secret door?" wondered Emily, "fancy going into a posh house like that with his dirty boots on!"

Sam wandered out into the corridor. In all of his eighty years he'd never set foot in the place but it felt like home. He sought out the red door but, to his annoyance, he discovered that it was securely locked from the inside. Some things never change. Why can't he be allowed to go out into the garden?

He produced his trusty penknife from his pocket and began to put to use all those tricks he'd learnt during the War. A mortice five lever deadlock was no match for Sam's skills. In a matter of minutes he slipped out of the door and into the garden without anybody seeing him.

The walled garden was still an abundance of flowers, trees and luscious green grass. Perhaps because he was forbidden to go there, it made it seem all the more wonderful. Suddenly Sam wheeled round.

"Come on *young*, Sam," barked Harold. His silver hair and grey moustache were unchanged. "I've told you before, Mr Forrester doesn't want you playing out here. Don't let me catch you in here ever again," he warned.

Sam watched Harold go into Beaven House through the red door. Curiously it was left open as if waiting for Sam to follow. He felt as though he might never see the garden again. He looked round and to his delight he saw Emily waiting for him by the side gate. Some things never change, only this time the two children would never have to leave the garden ever again.

Roger's Match **

The rain hammered incessantly against Roger MacKinnon's windscreen. Black clouds had gathered overhead, squeezing out what little daylight remained. The morbid silence, within the car, was suddenly broken by Roger's digital watch signalling 3 p.m. Wally sighed. That was it. Until then they'd clung to the hope that a passing motorist would stop and rescue them in their hour of need. What a marvellous day it would have been! But now it was too late; any hopes of making it to the match had vanished.

Wally rummaged around in his sports bag and, with a flourish, produced two cans of strong beer, like a magician, pulling rabbits out of a hat. The two friends set about demolishing the beer which they'd been saving for the match. Wally's whimsical comments about wizard brew and raising their spirits fell somewhat flat with Roger. He considered himself a conscientious sportsman and would not normally let a drop pass his lips, but, this was a special sad occasion.

Their local non-league team, Westport Wanderers, had reached the third round of the F A Cup proper for the first time in their history. They were playing the giants from the Premier League that day in front of a sell out crowd. But there would be two empty seats, Roger's car had run out of petrol in the middle of nowhere and there was no help in sight.

Roger was still furious with Pete. This was not the first time this sort of thing had happened. And Roger cursed his car. If only it could have spluttered on for a few miles more. It was all his wife's fault. Margaret would insist on them doing their weekly shopping on the Friday night. That meant traipsing across town to Calways. Needless to say, there was no where to fill up and Roger hadn't planned on using the car that weekend anyway.

It all began three weeks ago. Roger was in his study which was awash with red and white and the wall paper was completely hidden by football souvenirs and momentous. The draw had just been announced and Roger was feeling elated that his team were going to play at home to one of the big boys. It had prompted him to get out his entire collection of football programmes and other paraphernalia dating back to the year dot. Any excuse was good excuse. He kept his programmes in meticulous order. At the last count he'd three full scrap books of press cuttings including the the Infamous Goalpost Collapsing Incident of 1964.

"What are we going to do now, then? Sit here all day!" moaned a disgruntled Wally.

"We'll have to sit here at least until the rain eases off," replied a subdued Roger. "I wonder how the Reds are doing...?"

"Don't. Leave it out. I don't even wanna think about it..." Wally groaned.

There was a slight pause. Roger idly drummed his fingers on the dashboard.

"Margaret would have the last laugh if she could see us now," he remarked.

He remembered now putting down his scrapbook to go and see what his wife had wanted.

"Wonderful news, Roger. Sally's getting married and we're all invited," Margaret had announced happily.

There was nothing like a wedding to put Margaret in a good mood, but Roger was momentarily at a loss as to whom Sally was.

"You know, Sally," she'd said a little exasperated, "June's eldest daughter. She's getting married at St. Andrews Church in three weeks time - that will be the 17th."

"Oh, that Sally!" he'd muttered, not really that interested. "I won't be able to go anyway, I'm going to the football. The Wanderers are in the third round of the F A Cup. This is one match I'm not going to miss."

This wasn't what she'd wanted to hear. How humiliated she would feel having to tell Sally that Roger would not be going because of a lousy football match. How could he be so selfish? After all, it was his goddaughter's wedding he'd be missing. It didn't matter what she said, Roger had already made up his mind.

The acrid smell of Wally's cheap cigars disturbed Roger's reverie. He looked up to see Wally's grubby index finger inscribing the words "we're on our way to Wembley", in reverse, in the condensation on the windscreen.

"What yer think yer doing, Wally?" said Roger critically.

"I can't get my pocket radio to work in here. What happened to your car radio? Wally asked.

"I had it pinched, don't you remember? When we were away last season playing that team down at the gas works." Roger told him.

"Your lad's a whizz with cars, can't he fix you up with something?" Wally suggested.

Wally passed Roger another can of beer from his rapidly dwindling supply. Wally gulped down his beer and belched ostentatiously.

"Coming down the club on Wednesday?" Wally asked, "They've just had the tables redone. We could have a few frames - if we can get on a table that is."

"No, I don't think so, the place is full of kids these days," Roger replied. "Anyway, I've got to take Margaret out to dinner that night. It's our wedding anniversary."

He remembered how Margaret had snapped at him.

"I suppose you'll conveniently forget our wedding anniversary again, just like you did last year!"

That had hurt.

"I won't forget, I promise you," Roger had bleated, "I've written it down in my diary. It's the Wednesday after the match. I'll take you out to The Beeze Neeze, if you like. It's a promise!"

Slipping on his jacket and red and white scarf, he'd nipped out of the door whilst she was still drawing breath.

Luckily, he'd already arranged to meet Wally down at their local. When he'd arrived the atmosphere was in full swing with Wally leading the chanting. It had seemed like the whole pub was going to the big match and judging by the state of euphoria you'd have thought they'd already won the cup.

The tension was almost too much for Roger. He was paranoid that somehow his tickets might be invalid. His mind had conjured up all sorts of scenarios involving forged and incorrectly dated tickets. Every now and then he'd unzipped his jacket pocket and had carefully removed his ticket from inside, just to check that all the details were correct. That was three weeks ago now and Margaret still hadn't forgiven Roger for his treachery.

This morning Donald, their son, had called to take his mother to the church.

"You look very smart, Donald," she'd said with a smile. "Not like one person I could mention."

Her eyes had gazed across at Roger standing there dressed top to bottom in red and white.

"You look very nice too, Mother," remarked her thoughtful son. "What's all this then, Dad? You're not going dressed like that are you?"

"Your father's isn't coming; your father's going to a football match," Margaret spat.

Donald didn't have the slightest interest in football whatsoever and so despite his father's feeble protestations, the cup tie was of no significance to him.

"Look!" said Roger trying to make amends, "I'll come along to the reception after the match, if you like!"

Margaret had had more than a few words to say about that. She had got gingerly into her son's car being very careful not to crease her nice new blue dress she'd bought especially for the wedding. She'd checked with Sally's mother, Doris, to make sure they wouldn't be wearing the same colours. It was important for the bride's mother to stand out from the rest she'd humbly thought. Roger had ignored all her attempts to make him feel guilty. Nothing was going to upset his day. Pete would be there any minute and they would be off to the match. What a wonderful day it was going to be. He'd imagined the Wanderer's centre forward scoring the winner with just a few minutes to the final whistle.

Time had passed by, there had been no sign of Pete when Wally walked up the drive looking worried.

"Where's Pete?" Wally had asked.

"Don't know," Roger had replied anxiously, "pop round to his house and see what's up."

No sooner had Wally left, than the phone rang. It was Pete to say that he was very sorry but he wouldn't be able to come to the match. He had to take his mother to hospital. She was very ill and there was no possibility of Pete leaving her side. Not expressing any sympathy for Pete's unfortunate news, Roger had slammed down the phone and rushed outside to find Wally returning up the drive.

"Pete can't come," Roger had shouted in a panic, "we'll have to go in my car."

The worst of the storm had passed over by 4 p.m. Roger watched two trickles of rain race each other down the windscreen. Wally drained the last few drops from his can. They realised they couldn't sit there all night, so Roger produced an ordnance survey map from the glove compartment. He concluded that if they walked across the field opposite they should come to a village.

The two friends approached the muddy track which purported to be a public footpath although you would never have known it. Their bright red and white figures looked incongruous against the dull grey skyline.

They squelched on into the next field and by now they were both caked in mud. Wally remarked that he would rather be doing circuit training than having to put up with these conditions. It was dark by now and they were both feeling the cold. They were relieved to see a light in the distance. As they made their way towards it, they could hear the repetitive thud of a disco beat. They'd stumbled upon a village hall.

The two mud splattered friends went inside and to Roger's surprise they realised they'd gate crashed Sally's wedding reception. The hall was bedecked with streamers and balloons; a giant banner with the words, "Congratulations Sally and Rob", was emblazoned across the wall behind the disco. It seemed as if the World and his wife, all dressed in their best bib and tucker, had turned out to fete the happy couple. Roger and Wally felt a distinctly unhappy couple. Roger peered across the room and Margaret glared back. She was plainly not amused.

Just then, Roger felt a hand on his elbow and he was gently steered in the direction of changing rooms. He and Wally were furnished with clean clothes by Sally's father who politely insisted they put them on.

The smell of liniment hung in the air which seemed strangely welcoming to them.

"Didn't we play here last season?" asked Wally, "I'm sure I've been in here before".

"You have. We played here last season in the Cup, Barnfied Athletic, we won 2-1, don't you remember?" Roger informed him.

"I didn't play any cup games last season, I was out with a ham string," insisted Wally.

"No you did that later, you definitely played here last season. I know that for a fact, you gave away the penalty".

They continued their banter until Sally's father ushered them back into the hall. A sumptuous buffet had been provided for the benefit of the guests and no sooner had the cling film been removed than Wally dived in, piling his plate with vol–au–vents, quiche lorraine, sandwiches and anything else he could get his hands on.

If Sally's parents had harboured any ideas of genteel maiden aunts clutching paper plates waiting patiently in line, it would surely been destroyed by Wally's intervention which had turned the whole thing into a gastronomic free–for–all.

The guests made their way to the tables whilst Roger attempted to balance a paper plate on his knees. As he lunged for his sausage on a stick, he almost dropped the lot when he was startled by a screech of feedback from the disco's P.A. Sally's father had attempted to make a speech but it ended up an unintelligible mush which left the guests nonplussed. It suddenly struck Wally that the football results would be on the radio at that time. Taking his radio from his pocket he switched it on and held it to his ear. Suddenly he cried out, rudely interrupting Sally's father's speech.

"What is it, Wally, did we win?" asked Roger anxiously.

"It was called off due to a waterlogged pitch. They've re–scheduled the match for next week and they say we'll be able to use our tickets for that," announced Wally.

Roger and Wally jumped for joy, doing a jig around the dance floor much to the embarrassment of the wedding guests. What elation. What a stroke of luck. Just when they thought all was lost things had turned out well after all.

"Just think," beamed Roger, "we'll be there with all the lads from the Rose and Crown. We won't miss it this time. When did you say it was again, Wally?'

"It'll be a 7.30 kick-off, this Wednesday the 21st," Wally told him.

How was Roger going to explain that to Margaret?

Rufus

Hi. My name's Rufus and my owner has recently become a vegetarian and gone green. He's decided that I should also live on a meatless diet, so gone are the days of the traditional canned dog food. My diet now consists of some strange vegetable and cereal mixture specifically designed for dogs. I don't know what dogs they had in mind but it doesn't please my appetite! He never asked me if I wanted to be a vegetarian. He just assumed that I would, so I had no choice. Now don't get me wrong, I'm quite happy to be veggie, but why can't I have what he has instead of this strange mixture? The food he now eats makes my mouth water, but unless I can manage to look at him with wanting eyes, I don't get any. Last night he did give me some of his dinner and it was delicious. Tonight though, I sat and watched him eat that lovely looking vegetable curry and not one morsel did he give me.

"You can't have any of this, Rufus," he said, "it'll be too rich for you."

He's settled down to another boring evening reading his book. He's so set in his ways; it's as much as I can do to get him to take me for a walk. Tonight he won't even do that and I'm so bored. I want some fun and excitement just like all other young dogs. Now I've just had an idea. Any minute now he'll pop out to the kitchen to make himself a cup of tea. Yes, there he goes, regular as clockwork. Here's my chance, I'll hide his book somewhere so that he has a job finding it. Now where can I put it? No, not there, that's too easy. Ah, just here will do, he won't find it there in a hurry. He's coming back, must pretend nothing's amiss.

"Rufus, have you seen my book?"

I'm not telling him where it is, he'll have to find it himself. This is fun, he's just looked to see if the book has slipped behind the back of the chair. I've got him puzzled now, he can't work it out. Off he goes to the kitchen again; he won't find it there! Back he comes, has a good look round the room, no still can't see it. Oh, he's given up and picked up the newspaper instead. No fun at all. Think I'll go for a walk out into the hallway and chase my tail for something to do. Hello, somebody's just popped a leaflet through the letter box. We get loads of them around here, anything from double glazing to advertisements for potted plants. Hello, what's this though? Looks interesting!

"Bored, lonely, unattached?" That's me all right. "We are a specialised friendship agency that has brought happiness to many people." Sounds good, but what about dogs? "For a small introductory fee we could put you on the road to happiness and fulfilment with the person of your dreams." Hum, I wonder if there's a lady out there who would take him on? She might have a nice looking bitch! Worth a try anyway. If I place it on his lap he might read it.

"What've you got there, Rufus? What's this, a specialised friendship agency! Whatever next!"

I can't have this, he's just nodded off to sleep and not given it a second thought. I've got to get him interested in it somehow.

A week's just gone past and to my amazement his membership details for that friendship agency has just arrived in the post. Things are looking up; there's hope for us yet. Thing to do now is to have a browse through the ladies profiles and pick out a suitable partner for him. Now let's see. "Jane. Five foot ten and fifteen stone.." No she won't do, she'd crush him to death! This one looks more promising. "Sally, five feet five and nine stone. Attractive. Loves to dance the night away at discos and parties." No, on second thoughts, he'd never last the pace. Now this one sounds just right. "Janet, five feet five and eight stone. Loves reading poetry. Prefers a quiet night in to going out." She sounds as boring as he does, but here's the best bit. " She's a committed vegetarian and loves animals, especially dogs." Perhaps she'll do something to improve my dinners.

So I've decided she's the one, she's just the one for him. All I have to do now is draw his attention to her profile.

Believe or not, he contacted Janet and they're well suited. They both sit with their heads in books

188

all evening. But not me, she brings Honey with her and she's taken a shine to me I can tell. I've plucked up the courage to ask her out tonight. I haven't decided if we'll sniff round the dustbins or go for a run around the garden.

Oh and one other thing. The food's much improved since Janet arrived on the scene. Honey and I enjoy the same vegetarian cuisine as they do, except that we don't get wine with our dinner. But, we're working on it. "Ruff, ruff!"

The Runabout **

"Can you take that on the portable, please, darling?" John called out. "I can't stop now I've got to get this report done tonight." At the sixth time of ringing he grabbed the receiver. "Sue, It's for you!" he snapped.

"I'm not in," she called down the stairs.

"It's your Aunt Maggie" he shouted back.

Aunt Maggie and Sue were very close; more like sisters despite the age gap. Sue breezed into the room.

"Oh, why didn't you say. I'm always glad to talk to Aunt Maggie,"

John immersed himself once more in his portfolio. As a Regional Sales Manager he was expected to take his work home with him. Half–way through his sales forecast, he felt a tap on his shoulder.

"John," Sue asked, handing him a cup of coffee.

"Not now, I'm busy."

She continued: "You know that car you promised to buy me?"

"Yes, all right, leave it with me, I'll get it sorted soon."

"The thing is, you don't need to bother now. You see, Aunt Maggie has been to see the doctor and he says although she's over the worst of it now, she ought to give up driving."

"A good job too," he said dryly, "her and that Austin A40 are a menace to the road."

Sue paused to reconsider her tactics: "It was so nice of her, I could hardly refuse."

"Hardly refuse what?"

"Since she won't be able to use it anymore she insists I should have it. It'll be very useful as a runabout."

There was a moments pause. Then the balloon went up

"No way!" he shouted. "You're not driving that old wreck. I'd be the laughing stock of the whole street; Bill would never let up. We'd have to move. I couldn't stand the embarrassment!"

Poor John. Despite the fact that Aunt Maggie had kept the car in mint condition, his reaction was exactly as Sue had expected.

"Don't be such a snob, John. What does it matter what the neighbours think? Anyway, what's wrong with the car?"

"What's wrong? What's wrong?" he shouted. "Give me a break!"

The argument raged. Aunt Maggie had been very good to both of them over the years, Sue knew that John wouldn't wish to appear ungrateful and offend her. Once Sue had got him to accept this fact then he bowed to the inevitable.

He got up early next morning and went outside whilst Sue got on with the household chores. She wondered what he was up to; she could hear his car coming and going. Eventually he came inside with a smile on his face.

"That's a good job well done," he told her. "I've cleared the garage and taken all the rubbish down to the dump. Now there's enough room for both my car and the A40."

"You've changed your tune, haven't you? When are we going to pick it up?"

"Ten o'clock tonight."

"But it'll be dark then," she said looking at him and then realised why. "Oh, I get it, you think you can sneak it into the garage without anyone seeing it, don't you?"

And she was right. As he steered the car nervously onto the newly gravelled driveway he was caught in the glare of the automatic security light. If that wasn't enough the squealing of the garage doors was so loud it could have woken the whole neighbourhood. In a cold sweat he looked around to see if anybody was about.

"What on earth are you doing?" Sue shouted from the A40.

"Shh! Keep it quiet will you. There's not enough room for both cars," he hissed. "Put that old heap in for now; I'll sort it out tomorrow."

"Of course there's enough room," she scoffed going into the garage.

To John's horror, Sue started moving the mower and garden tools about making a loud din in the process.

"Oh no, it's Bill from next door." John rushed over to him. "Evening, Bill, how's things?"

"Just taking the dog for a walk. What you doing out?"

"Oh nothing, nothing," replied John trying to sound innocent, "just getting a breath of fresh air. I'll walk with you. Going this way are you?"

John led Bill away from the scene and indicated behind his back, to Sue, for the A40 to go in the garage. When they were out of sight Sue started the engine, switched on the lights and drove in. Shutting the doors they squeaked again and she noticed one or two neighbours peering out of their windows. To Sue's annoyance, John kept the A40 locked away in the garage. He was determined to keep it there, out of sight.

"Aunt Maggie's coming to tea on Sunday," Sue told John when he came home from work one evening.

"Oh great, Sue! I need that like a hole in the head. You know I've got a pile of work to do. She's a sweet old lady but not this weekend!"

"You've got to relax sometime. Anyway she won't be in your way. I promised I'd take her for a ride in the A40."

John was furious with Sue. He'd achieved a high standard of living for both of them. Everything he'd brought to the home was of the highest quality and taste. He was well respected in the street. This would make a fool of him he told her.

Aunt Maggie arrived for tea that Sunday. Every time she mentioned the A40 John quickly changed the subject.

"Be a dear and do the dishes, John, will you," Aunt Maggie politely ordered.

She had that knack of organising everyone around her without appearing to be obtrusive. John dutifully did as he was told, but kept the door ajar, hanging on their every word.

"Ready for a ride in your old car, Aunt Maggie?" Sue asked presently.

"Ready when you are."

John heard this and let out a silent scream. He thought he had to try and stop them or the neighbours would know everything. He heard the front door close as he struggled to take off the rubber gloves.

Finally he got his hands free but then carelessly cut his finger on a sharp knife. He scurried about the kitchen looking for some plasters but unable to find some he rushed outside.

"Sue, quick!" he shouted showing her his finger. "I cut it on that blasted self-sharpening knife of yours. I told you we should have bought a dish washer but you wouldn't listen."

"Oh let me see," she tutted, taking hold of his hand.

194

"You'll need stitches in that," declared Aunt Maggie taking a look for herself.

In keeping with his Company status, John had recently taken delivery of a brand new 2.3 litre fuel injected automatic saloon. Unfortunately, Sue had only previously driven a car with manual gears. She hastily pressed her foot firmly on the accelerator and drove straight into the wall with a loud crash. John was mortified.

"Well have to take you in my old car," smiled Aunt Maggie who found the whole situation amusing. "I'll drive, Sue, you don't look in a fit state to take the wheel."

Sue was shaken by the incident and John's constant ranting and raving didn't help matters. They both protested to Aunt Maggie that she shouldn't be driving but their pleas fell on deaf ears. As Aunt Maggie reversed the A40 out of the garage John looked around to see if any of the neighbours were watching.

The car sped off down the road as John and Sue sat in the back fearing for their lives. Aunt Maggie drove like a maniac, screeching around corners not bothering to change gear. Miraculously they arrived at the hospital after somehow avoiding a head on collision with an ambulance. John received several stitches to his finger and was relieved when the doctor gave him the okay to drive.

"I'll drive back," John said tactfully, "I'm dying to have a go in this."

He couldn't believe he'd said that. The last thing on earth he wanted to do was to drive the A40. Yet there he was driving up his street and standing outside was Bill cutting the hedge.

"Oh no, total humiliation!"

John quickly parked in the garage hoping Bill hadn't see the car. Bill came straight over and stood in the garage doorway.

"Hello, there," Bill called out, "your new car is it?" he laughed.

John crouched down in the drivers seat in a vain attempt not to be seen. Bill knocked on the side window and reluctantly John got out of the car.

"She's a beauty isn't she?" declared Bill admiring the A40. "Where did you get this from? You lucky devil, John, I've always fancied a vintage car."

John's head spun. He couldn't believe his luck. He hadn't realised what he'd got.

"Not bad is she. Just a little runabout for Sue, you know. Want a look under the bonnet, Bill?"

Sue and Maggie may as well have been invisible for all the attention they received. They both went into the house for a cup of tea and left John to play to the gallery.

Snapshot *

I don't think I was pushy, was I? I only wanted you to be successful, what woman wouldn't want that for her husband. Why did you have to do it? And how dare you see that woman behind my back. All that mess - I must get this cleared up.

"Can I help you, madam?"

Oh, quick, where's the receipt? I'm sure I put it in my bag here somewhere - yes, here it is - take it. I can't wait to see the look on your face when I show you these pictures. What will you have to say for yourself then?

"Here you are, madam, see you again next week, ha ha".

Cheeky bitch. I expect she's been looking at them. So I shall put these pictures in my bag where nobody can get at them and I shan't touch them again until I'm safely in the car.

You never took me to that restaurant, but you took her. Where's all the money coming from, Bill? We've been married two years and I'm still waiting for new carpets which we'd agreed to. Scheming Cow! Well now I have all the proof I need.

Right. I'll just get my glasses from the glove compartment. What's this - the Car Insurance? It's still in your name, Bill, I must do something about that now you've gone.

197

That's her, I'd recognise her anywhere - even by candle light. All dolled up, like a tart on her night off. But just a minute. Who's that man with her? That's not Bill. I was there; I caught them at it. So I went into that restaurant and took these pictures myself. But you're not in any of them, Bill, I don't understand.

"Hello, rotten day, isn't it? Been to the shops, have you"?

That's all I need. Nosey neighbours. She was the first to gossip after it happened. What a shock I got when I came home and found you. What a selfish thing to do, Bill.

Where's my key? These free newspapers are a nuisance piling up behind the door. They never bring me good news. I'll put these useless pictures in the drawer with the others. All those photographs and not one of them of you, Bill.

This house needs a good clean; the front room hasn't been touched since you went. It's out of bounds now.

Who was that man in there? All that mess. It looked nothing like you, Bill. You'd polished off the rest of the whisky from the drinks cabinet, though. You even wore that suit you'd bought for Rosemary's wedding last year - but now it was covered in blood - wherever did you get a shotgun from, Bill?

That's where I first saw that Scheming Cow - at your funeral. She's trying to take you away from me, isn't she? Rosemary was on the phone again this morning. She's still begging me to move away from here. Silly girl, I couldn't possibly do that! What would you say when you came home, Bill?

Stolen Love

Brian nervously opened the door. He was wary of his wife at the best of times but on this occasion he had every reason to be. He'd rehearsed in his mind over and over again what he would say to her. He tried various ways but none of the words seemed to sound right.

"What time do you call this?" his wife, Doreen yelled at him as he entered the kitchen. "Your dinner's ruined. I don't know why I bother."

He started to shake. She was already in a mood and he hadn't even told her the bad news yet. His words became all jumbled up in his mind. He stammered and spluttered but they just wouldn't come out.

"For goodness sake don't just stand there mumbling," she hissed, "get your coat off and eat your dinner, what's left of it."

He sat down to eat the burnt offerings that lay before him. He had to tell her now and get it over and done with. The longer he left it the worst it would be for him. Besides, the police said they'd be round shortly.

"The car's been stolen,' he said eventually.

Doreen looked at him in amazement. She couldn't take in what he'd said.

"What do you mean the car's been stolen? How?"

"I came out of work and it was gone. I've phoned the police, they'll be here soon."

"The police! Here? Just look at this place, it's a mess. Never mind your dinner we've got to tidy up."

She snatched his plate from him and tipped his dinner into the swing bin. She shouted and cursed him; it was all his fault the car had been stolen.

A policeman and a female colleague arrived to take details of the car theft. Brian tried to be as helpful as he could. He explained that it would be difficult for him to get to work without his car as there were no trains and very few buses on his route.

It was then that Brian noticed that Doreen was paying a lot of attention to the handsome young PC. He felt awkward and didn't quite know where to look. He caught the WPC's eye and she smiled thinly back at him. He felt sorry for her; she seemed more embarrassed than he was.

"We'll I think we've got all the details we need for now, sir," the WPC blurted out whilst rustling her papers. "I'll make sure we stay in touch until we find the car. In the meantime I do hope you manage to get to work all right."

Brian felt reassured. The WPC had made him feel much happier about the situation.

As soon as the officers had left Doreen shouted and screamed at Brian that, as usual, he had been so indecisive and had given the police nothing to go on. Getting to work without the car was totally irrelevant as far as his wife was concerned. He wanted to confront her about her flirting but he just couldn't face it.

Each day he managed to get to work by bus but this entailed an extra hour's journey each way. After two weeks the car hadn't been traced and he wasn't having much luck with his insurance claim.

"It's entirely your fault. You should ring the insurance company and tell them exactly what you want," Doreen shouted at him.

"No luck with your car?" Brian's boss asked him one Friday afternoon.

"No."

"Brian, can you do something for me? I've got to get this tender to Eddingtons today. It's on the way home for you isn't it? If I arrange a taxi would you take it for me? Get the taxi to take you home afterwards. You can have the rest of the day off."

Brian was very grateful to his boss, he was glad to go home early for a change. When he got home, he saw a police car in his drive. Perhaps they've found the car he thought. He opened his front door and called out as usual. He went in the kitchen to see if Doreen was there but there didn't appear to be anybody at home. Suddenly somebody hurried down the stairs and slammed the front door. He peered out of the window and to his surprise he saw the policeman, in a state of undress, scurrying to his car.

Doreen did not try deny it. It had been going on ever since his car had been stolen.

"Out!" he shouted. "Get out and don't ever come back."

He packed some of her clothes into a suitcase and threw it outside the front door. She calmly picked up the case and walked away with her nose in the air.

It felt good. At last he'd asserted himself and he wouldn't take her back. The policeman was welcome to her. The next day he took the rest of her things and dumped them at the police station. Later the WPC called at his house.

"Oh," he said, "is it about my wife's things?"

"No, they've been passed onto her," she replied hesitantly, "it's about something else."

"It's nice to see you again. What can I do for you?"

"We'll, we've found your car and there's not a scratch on it. It's down at the station. I can give you a lift now, if you like." she asked hopefully.

"I can't at the moment but could I pick it up later?"

She looked disappointed as she turned and walked towards her panda car. She switched on the engine and was about to drive away when she heard a knock on her window.

"I've changed my mind," said Brian, getting into the car. "I'll accept your offer of a lift, on one condition."

"What's that?" she asked coyly.

"Would you have dinner with me this evening?" he asked hopefully.

"I"d love to," she said delighted.

204

The Stranger **

It was a hot summers day in July, two years ago. The stench from the river was particularly bad in the stifling heat. All forms of life in the river had ceased to exist since Bill Hobson had opened his chemical factory offering jobs for all. True, he did offer employment for some two hundred people but at a very high environmental cost. Few people realised what was really going on and there was no stopping Bill Hobson. He had money, power and influence.

As children played in the woods beside the stinking river, two squirrels did their best to scavenge for food amongst the dying trees. All along the banks of the river the vegetation was yellowing and shrivelled; no wildlife was welcome here. Then, out of nowhere, appeared a man. He was tall, had short dark hair and was quite slim. He wore a turquoise short sleeved shirt and a pair of black jeans. He carried a curious looking case, something like a Gladstone bag. He said nothing but just stood motionless, gazing at the lifeless river. Eventually, he sat down on a log and took out a Bible from his case and began to read. The children noticed him sitting there and being inquisitive wanted to know who he was and what he was doing.

"I've come to make the river better," he answered.

"Is it sick?" asked one child.

"Very sick", he replied thoughtfully.

A couple of days later news had reached Bill Hobson that there was somebody down by the river who seemed to be carrying out some sort of analysis. Bill was overweight, stocky and had a bushy red beard. He was a short tempered man and was angered to learn of this work because he had not been consulted. He resolved to go down to the river and confront this uninvited guest. Whenever he was holding one of these interviews he always took one of his minders with him.

"What do you think you're doing?" Bill demanded. "Who gave you permission to work on my land?"

The stranger rose, closed his Bible and stood looking firmly at Bill. He handed Bill an official looking piece of paper.

"I'm acting on behalf of your Government," announced the stranger, "I've been commissioned to investigate the condition of your rivers and lakes."

"Well, go and investigate somewhere else. 'Cos there ain't nothing wrong with this river." Bill shouted in defiance.

"Then there's nothing for you to worry about," replied the stranger.

"Now look here!" retorted Bill, "I'm warning you. If you cause me any trouble I'll be after you. Nobody's going to close my factory down."

The stranger raised his eyebrows: "What factory is that?" he asked.

"You know what I mean," Bill said, pointing his finger, "I know your sort and your sort's not wanted round here, especially foreigners. What are you? An Aussie or what?"

The stranger sat on the log: "I was born in South Africa but have travelled the World most of my life."

"We don't want interfering do–gooders like you around. Clear off!" shouted Bill.

The stranger opened up his Bible and began reading it once again. Bill turned and marched off back to his factory with his minder following. Bill was a hard, mean businessman and nobody was going to get in his way. He meant what he said. Anyone who had tried to cross him had always got more than they bargained for.

The following day our South African friend returned carrying his case. He took out some odd looking instruments and placed them in the river.

"What are you doing?" the children asked. "What are those funny looking things for?"

"I'm testing the river. I'm going to take some samples of it," he answered.

"What for?" the children asked.

He smiled: "I'm going to find out what's making the river sick."

"Will you give it some medicine?" asked a child, "I hate medicine. My mum gives it to me when I'm sick. It's horrible."

This started the children chattering about their maladies and medicines. As they skipped away, the stranger just smiled and continued about his work.

The stranger continued, each day, to take samples from the river, except, that is, on a Sunday. On that day he sat for hours engrossed in his Bible. Although he read his Bible every day; on Sunday he never seemed to do anything else.

Apart from the children and Bill Hobson nobody ever spoke to him. The villagers thought him strange and couldn't understand why he spent so much time just taking samples of the river. What did he hope to achieve? The river was polluted, they knew that. But so what? It didn't affect them. Besides many people in the village had good jobs at the factory and it wouldn't do to upset Bill Hobson.

Over the next few weeks Bill became increasingly agitated by the stranger's presence. The guy was a real thorn in his side. He couldn't shake him off. Every time he tried talking sense to him he just buried his head in his Bible. But Bill had people to see and deadlines to meet; he was a businessman. He couldn't waste any more time on him, he had to go. The question was how? He couldn't buy him off. So there was nothing else for it, he went down to the river with one of his minders.

"Okay. That's it I've had enough!" he shouted at the stranger, "people are talking. They're saying that you reckon I've poisoned the river. I'm telling you to leave now whilst you're still in one piece."

The stranger shook his head. He picked up his Bible.

"Don't think you can hide behind that book," warned Bill." My friend here is an Atheist, aren't you Sam?"

Sam nodded. He was big and muscular with an evil look in his eye. The stranger took no notice, sat down and began to read the Bible. Sam rolled up his sleeves, clenched tight his massive fist and threw a punch. With amazing strength the stranger caught hold of Sam's wrist and squeezed it tightly. Sam yelled out in pain as he was forced to his knees.

"All right, you win this time," yelled Bill, "but I'll be back!"

Bill was as good as his word. He held a meeting and explained to his workers that the stranger at the river was trying to get the factory closed down. Cleverly, Bill whipped up the resentment of his workforce. The angry mob marched down to the river. What could the stranger do against two hundred angry men? In that mood they might take the law into their own hands. When they reached the river the stranger was waiting, Bible in hand. Bill and the angry mob stopped ten yards short of him.

"This is your last chance, foreigner, go or die!" warned Bill.

The crowd roared. The stranger held up his arms and waited until the crowd quietened.

"Friends," said the stranger, "I shall be leaving here today."

The crowd shouted their approval but he silenced them.

"I know you are all worried about your jobs, but I'm sure your concern for your health and that of your families is greater. Nothing can live in this river. It has been polluted by extremely toxic chemicals produced by your factory."

"That's a lie", shouted Bill.

The crowd began shouting, but again the stranger regained their attention.

"I think you should know that Mr Hobson owned a factory in North America some five years ago. He polluted the lakes and rivers with his chemical waste. He claimed the chemicals would do no harm. Five years ago, to this day, three hundred people died as a result of poisoning after chemicals had infiltrated the drinking water system."

"That's enough, do you hear, it's all lies," shouted Bill desperately.

"Shut up Bill", somebody shouted. "Let him finish."

The stranger held up copies of newspaper reports about the disaster in America. The factory had closed down and Bill had fled America to avoid prosecution. He changed his name and came to Britain to start up in business, managing to keep the incident in America a secret.

As he finished speaking the police and a government official arrived with a court order to close the factory down. It was the end of the road for Bill Hobson. Just then one of the villagers noticed the stranger's picture in the American newspaper.

"That can't be him," said another, "it says he was one of the people who died of poisoning from the water supply. His wife and three children also died."

"If ain't him it's certainly the spitting image," replied the first villager.

As Bill Hobson was led away, the government official turned to thank the stranger for his work, but he had gone. He had disappeared as mysteriously as he had arrived. Then the official noticed something on a log. He went over and picked it up. It was the Bible.

Under The Bright Blue Sky **

"You do realise that the sky is blue out there don't you?" Donna offered.

"Yes, I did read that somewhere," Fairfax replied, "but only on a fine day. Otherwise, when it's dull, clouds cover the sky."

"Clouds?" she queried. "Clouds of gas?"

"No water vapour, I believe," he answered. "The clouds go on for miles and miles, you know."

Donna leapt and started waving her arms around, ranting and raving that she could change the World single handed. She was no beauty, with her tatty mane of copper coloured hair and her funny little button nose, but he loved her. He'd loved her ever since he'd laid eyes on her.

They'd had their arguments, like all couples do, but there was one thing he would always be grateful to her for. She'd made him accept himself for what he was. She was just like him - she was orange.

"Look, eight out of ten people in here are too old to have children, right. And over half the population are physically incapable, so it doesn't look good for the future, does it?" rattled Donna.

"What doesn't?" murmured Fairfax, half listening.

"The future of the Human Race," Donna replied flopping down by his side. "The next generation - our children."

"Doesn't stop us trying, does it?" quipped Fairfax, grabbing Donna round the waist. With a giggle, they performed a roly-poly locomotion across the plastic grass.

"It's one thing they don't stop us doing in here," Donna laughed.

Fairfax agreed: "We've been coming here for three months now and they haven't caught us yet."

Donna pulled him close. He could feel her heart beating like a hammer and their mouths kissed hungrily.

It wasn't the sight of their teenage passion that kept other citizens of The Dome from the park. Every day, before noon and until about three, everyone would descend to the Lower Levels, but Fairfax and Donna, curiously, never felt the need to join them. Donna thought it was a throw back to the old days outside when it would be too dangerous to risk the sun's rays. Nowadays, it was hotter still, but the harmful ultra violet could never penetrate The Dome's defences.

"Let's go down to the Archive Centre," suggested Donna, "I've still got some research to do for my thesis."

She leapt up, smoothed down her clothes and held her hand out to Fairfax. He struggled to his feet, reluctantly. Another two hours and he would have to return to the lab; he'd much rather have her to himself.

Their stroll took them past the Municipal Council Offices where his father, Matthew Ellison, worked. The ugly array of brick and tile had changed little since the turn of the Century. Neither had the Administration; the laws were simple and few, there could be no room for dissent.

The Dome was originally an experimental biosphere commissioned over seventy years ago. Its structure was showing increasing signs of corrosion and more frequent repairs were needed. For the last three months water supplies had been disrupted due to mechanical problems with the pumping equipment. This had highlighted the chronic lack of spare parts and the difficulty in manufacturing new ones.

As they approached the Archive Centre, Donna spotted several drones cleaning graffiti off a wall. Fairfax pointed to them.

"I suppose that's the work of the League, is it?"

"I don't even know what it means!" replied Donna coyly.

"Exodus!" said Fairfax darkly. "You being of Irish stock, I would have expected you to know your Bible."

Finding the whole thing amusing, she stuck out her tongue and ran off across the concourse. He felt depressed. Although he loved her he didn't feel at all easy with some of her politics. He'd even wondered if their relationship was just a front; a way for these extremists to get to his father.

Matthew Ellison was an esteemed Biologist and Physicist, being one of the earliest colonists of The Dome over thirty years earlier. He continued to exert a profound influence on its affairs as he held Office as one of the Council Elders.

Fairfax's mother had died five years previously after a long illness, a fact his father found hard to come to terms with. Like many of the other Elders he too longed for the old world before The Collapse.

The famine and nuclear war had taken so many of his loved ones and laid down such a deadly legacy. The Human Race had salvaged what it could and taken sanctuary in The Dome.

Having tried various departments, Fairfax spotted Donna in the reference library, her diminutive figure surrounded by stacks of video cartridges, files and papers. She waved him over.

"You wouldn't believe it," groaned Fairfax. "I've forgotten my green disk and spent ten minutes arguing with those little tin gods in security. Luckily, Steadman came and cleared it for me." Donna's eyes remained fixed to the screen as the words "Twentieth Century Statesmen," appeared.

"How did you get in here, then?" Fairfax probed.

Donna gave him a saucy wink but it didn't register with him. He needed to talk seriously.

He went to the window, wiped it with his sleeve and looked out. He watched the jets of water arc through the air; the mist from the spume carried away to the vegetable gardens beyond. As the sprinkler cycle ended the canopy of water gently fell away.

Despite limiting themselves to growing cereals, fruit, root vegetables and soya and prohibiting all animals to help conserve water, the forecast wasn't good.

"Father says The Dome's days are numbered," he told Donna.

Her fingers paused then continued their dance across the keyboard.

"Well, we've been saying that for ages - have those sleepy old men just woken up to the facts?" she remarked drily.

Fairfax shouted: "How can you say that about the Elders? They've suffered just trying to keep this place going."

"Sounds like your father speaking," noted Donna.

"So what! All your cronies from the League ever do is bite the hand that feeds you. Our Elders are yesterday's men, that's all." He paused, as if he'd just realised what he'd said. "Times running out, Donna. What The Dome needs now is someone new with new ideas to lead us out of this mess."

She looked up at him, her champion, his face aglow.

"Now you're talking," she cheered.

Gathering up her files in a Hessian bag, she led him by the arm and pushed passed security who had come clanking in, lights a-flashing, to see what all the noise was about. Beyond the edge of the concourse they looked up at the giant hexagonal sections intermeshed over two hundred feet above them.

Donna broke the silence: "It was only supposed to be temporary. It'll be too late for most people now."

Fairfax wondered: "You don't think anyone could have survived out there do you?"

"Let's find out," challenged Donna. "Those friends of yours with strange looking eyes and extra fingers and thumbs may not be the freaks you think they are. I'm orange and none of my family were radioactive to my knowledge!"

It became clear to him in an instant. It was beyond co-incidence that their biologies matched. They were the answer to a world blistered by ozone depletion, fall-out and disease.

In his mind's eye he saw a future time: a little orange boy running out to play with all the other orange children. Their child had made lots of new friends, out there, under the bright blue sky.

Utopia Island

Thomas was panicking. Stuck in a traffic jam, he'd be late for work again. His mind was full of targets and deadlines. It would be another hard day at the office.

Seeing a sign for Utopia Island he found himself following its route. It lead him to the docks where he left his car and boarded the ferry for the short trip to the island.

On arrival he was greeted by Paul and Rosemary; two founder members of Utopia. As they showed him round they explained their principles to him. There was no money in circulation. Each occupant was provided with ample food and shelter as payment for their work.

Thomas felt a warm glow when he heard that nobody was under any pressure. Everybody was equal, there were no targets to achieve or deadlines to meet.

Doctors, dentists, tradesman and farmers had all settled there. What could Thomas offer the island? He was a good administrator and had experience in amateur dramatics. Perhaps he could start a theatre company providing free entertainment for all islanders. Instead of money, visitors would bring a gift of some kind - something that would be of service to everyone such as fuel or bedding.

It was decided that his new theatre company would perform plays that were no longer under copyright or ones he'd written himself, so there'd be no problems with royalties. He'd always fancied himself as a playwright.

Paul and Rosemary welcomed Thomas as a citizen of Utopia Island. He felt excited and much relieved that he was leaving the pressures of a materialistic world behind him.

Thomas was startled by the sound of a car horn; the lights had just changed to green. He was back to the targets and deadlines; it would be another hard day at the office.

Wedding Bells

"Wake up, Ray, wake up! Don't just lie there, we've got a wedding to go to, remember?"

Just look at him. Oh no, you can't can you? You're just reading this so you can't see his face and believe me, you don't know how lucky you are. I mean, what a state to get into, eh? Pale faced, bloodshot eyes and he calls that having a good time.

"That's what you're supposed to do on stag nights," he says, "you're supposed to get so drunk you can't stand up."

He'd never considered the sober option.

"Have a nice evening out, have a couple of drinks but don't over do it," I suggested.

The thought of having a pleasant evening, enjoying some good food in an amenable atmosphere just doesn't appeal to Ray. It's pathetic really, a twenty nine year old man coming on sixteen.

Now I was all for having the stag night on Thursday. At least then he would have had all day Friday to recover from his hangover. As it stands he's got to make himself presentable in front of the Vicar. Mind you, that's a laugh, it's difficult to say who was the more stoned last night. Ray or the Vicar, whom when we left him last night, was dancing on a table to the "Bat Out Of Hell" song.

So anyway, Ray had it his way and we had the stag night last night. Now me, not that I'm a party pooper or anything, but I stuck to halves of cider before moving onto orange juice. Ray, on the other hand, drank at least ten pints as well some wines and spirits. No wonder he spent the early hours of the morning with his head down the toilet. I lost count of the times he called out Huey's name and the toilet was flushed so many times it's a wonder the sewers aren't over flowing.

"Now come on, Ray, we're due at the alter soon. Now I know you'd rather be left to die peacefully in your bed and perhaps that's the more humane option. But I'm sorry old son, you have a responsibility to be there on time and on time you're gonna be."

You might think I'm rather harsh and that I should leave him in peace. Consider this though. It's a fine spring morning. The wedding is taking place in a beautiful three hundred year old church in the picturesque village of Hillingworth. It's a perfect setting for a perfect wedding. Now I'm not going let Dave spoil it all for Jennifer. If he doesn't turn up on time she'll give him what for, I can tell you. As the bride it's her privilege to be late, not his. It doesn't take much for Ray to wind Jenny up as it is. He will insist on calling her Jenny sometimes, just to make her angry.

"I was christened Jennifer and Jennifer is what I should be called," she's forever insisting.

I'm really glad you can't see this lump of dog's mess. That's a polite way of describing him but I refuse to swear on a day like this. That smile on his face will soon diminish when he realises what a headache he has. At least, if there's any justice in this World he'll have the worst headache imaginable.

Oh no. You wouldn't believe it, would you? He's only be sleeping in his wedding suit all night. Not only that but he's wearing his trousers the wrong way round. How anyone could mistake a wedding suit for a pair of pyjamas is beyond me. It's got more creases in it that the Oval Cricket Stadium and his shirt's got something down the front of it, it's quite disgusting.

"Come on, Ray, let's get your trousers on properly....No, Ray, I'm not a blondy-bender as you so crudely put it. You can't go out with your flies facing you backside. In any case, what happens when you want to go to the loo? What are you going to do then? If you don't want me to help you then you better put those trousers on properly within the next two minutes. Okay?"

I feel sorry for Jennifer, I really do. You wouldn't believe the trouble her parents have gone to over this wedding. Nothing too good or too much trouble to make their daughter's day anything but less than perfect. I can see it now. Everyone will be at the wedding bright as buttons. I know all the men will be very smart and the women will be beautifully dressed, though not as beautiful as Jennifer of course. Then there will be Ray, dressed as a tramp.

"I'm loosing patience with you, Ray. Just give me the ring and I'll wait outside."

This is the last straw, you know. If you've had any sympathy for Ray up until now you won't have when I tell you that he can't find the wedding ring. All I can get out of him was that he remembers opening up a jar of pickles last night and he seems to think he might of dropped the ring in it. He thinks it's just a joke.

"Don't worry," he's forever telling me. "I can handle, Jenny don't you worry."

She'll handle him all right. She'll kill him. Still, she should have listened to her mother. We both should have. Her mother was right. He's a lazy good for nothing.

"Now listen, Ray. If you don't find that wedding ring and pull yourself together I'll never speak to you again. Some best man you've turned out to be!"

When A Child Is Born

Dalia sat anxiously in the waiting room with her husband, Gardone. She stared at the drab wall paper that must have been at least forty years old. They'd always wanted a child but it had taken them all this time to get this far. At last the waiting was almost over - today they'd know their fate.

They'd been able to demonstrate their suitability as potential parents. They were both very intelligent and had Honours Degrees. Gardone was Headmaster at the local school whilst Dalia taught History.

The receptionist called their names and directed them down the corridor to Room Five. Their footsteps echoed as their shoes clomped against the wooden floor. Gardone held her hand. He knocked on the door.

"Come in," a voice commanded.

They entered and nervously sat down. An authoritative looking man looked up at them and managed a half smile.

"We have decided to accept your application to have a child. You may attempt to conceive as from today."

Dalia couldn't restrain her delight: "Oh thank you, thank you, thank you. You don't know what this means."

The man showed no humour: "I know only too well what this means. Are you sure you do?'

His question subdued Dalia's happiness. Gardone spoke for both of them.

"We realise what this means, sir. Despite everything we know it's the right decision."

The man nodded: "It's important for both of you to realise the consequences when a child is born." He paused for a moment. He looked Dalia in the eye. "Your mother is in full agreement?"

"Yes my mother understands. She's signed the consent form."

"Yes, madam, I have the papers in front of me. All the same, I have to be sure."

Gardone intervened: "Dalia's mother is a wonderful woman. She's prepared to do the same for Dalia as her mother did for her."

"Very well, I will make the arrangements when the time comes. There is one thing I must tell you. Even though she's the only surviving parent and although we are allowing this birth, I'm afraid you will not be able to have a second child. You will both be sterilised once you've had the baby."

They were disappointed to hear this news but they were grateful to the man. Many of their friends hadn't been so lucky.

They walked home. Nobody travelled by car or public transport any more save Royalty and a few important politicians. Even trains were now reserved for the privileged.

On returning home Gardone put on his overalls ready for his spare time job. Dalia kissed him.

"While you're out, I'll have my shower. Will you have yours tonight?"

Gardone shook his head. "I'm working on the Cleveland site tomorrow and pulling down that shopping centre is going to be dirty work. I'll have my shower after that."

"They should make allowances for you Gardone. They should let you have a shower more than once a week with all that dirty work you have to do. You shouldn't have to do it anyway, not a man in your position."

"Every able man has to do his share regardless of status, Dalia, you know that. The unemployed have to do it every day. Luckily my duties are only three times a week so at least I'll be clean until Tuesday."

"What's happening on Tuesday?"

"Azma Supermarket has been pulled down. Next job is to remove the foundations."

"Do they really think they can return the area to farm land?"

"That's the theory. The Government has plans to tear down some five hundred supermarkets and shopping centres. They estimate that in ten years time there will be twenty more farms than there are now."

"I wish I'd lived in the Twentieth or Twenty First Century. I would have done something to stop the destruction."

Gardone smiled: "Always the idealist."

"Yes well, many environmentalists warned Governments against over population and the concrete jungle. The endless motorways that created endless traffic jams. Global warming. Industrial pollution. They were all warned but they just didn't listen.

"Yes, I know you've said: 'Human Rights, The Road Lobby and Religious Argument had had their say and now the Devil has had his.' I'm not one of your pupils, Dalia, I'm well aware of the situation. But there's hope. Open spaces and green fields are making a come-back."

Dalia nodded in agreement. She was just sad that it had taken so long for the World Powers to realise their folly. She worried for the sort of life her child would lead.

It was too late for the cat or dog. The cows that once grazed in the fields were now a distant memory. All animals had been obliterated in Man's desperate attempt to survive. Her child would have to be content with the History books.

Cattle were the first to be terminated. The Prime Minister of the day had declared.

"Cattle give off methane gas which is ten times more damaging than carbon dioxide. Their slurry is poisoning our water supplies. We have decided to eliminate these animals."

Later, in desperation, all animals were slaughtered in an attempt to conserve food supplies. The daily diet now depended on crops that required little water.

Dalia's mother, Henta, was delighted to hear of Dalia and Gardone's good news. She hoped Dalia would fall pregnant soon for she didn't want the uncertainty to linger on.

Henta's wishes were eventually answered and Dalia gave birth to Grear, a beautiful and healthy girl. They were overjoyed.

"Oh mother isn't she wonderful."

"Yes dear. I will give my life gladly."

Dalia tears of joy had turned to sadness. Henta cuddled her granddaughter before handing the smiling baby back to her crying mother.

"Don't cry for me, daughter. One day you'll do the same for Grear as she probably will for her child."

The authorities took Henta away and terminated her life. But Dalia had accepted it. She knew what happened when a child is born.

When I Propose *

It's that sparkle in your eyes. It gets me every time. How could anyone possibly refuse you? Those beautiful, beautiful eyes. Don't tease me. Anyway, nothing's going to stop us now.

Look at the mess in this bathroom cabinet. I cannot believe the amount of stuff Viv collects. It's like a tart's boudoir in here. Where are my disposable razors? Here they are. I'd better use a fresh one. I need to be at my sharpest tonight. Ha ha.

Tilt your head up slightly. That's better, into the light, so that I can have a good look at you. Your skin's so soft - just like a woman's. Most men would want that, wouldn't they? I don't want to nick that tiny mole again. It bled for hours last time.

No, the more I worry, the worse it will be. The only way is to treat the whole thing as pure routine. Just as I'll treat the whole evening. Once tonight's out of the way things will be different.

Remember the day I first met Elizabeth? As always, on a Monday night, I was on my way to Lennie's Wine Bar. It's been a popular haunt for guys for several years now. I like to go there. There's never any trouble. It's discreet and it's a place I can go where nobody's going to recognise me.

As it was, I never made it to the wine bar that night. Elizabeth stepped into the road and almost ended up underneath my car. I swerved, pretty dammed skilfully I thought, to avoid an accident. Yet she just stood in the road screaming at me. She was clearly in a state of shock, poor thing. I had no choice, so I offered to take her to hospital.

According to her, of course, it was all my fault. Elizabeth was making a performance out of it. I had to use a little bit of old fashioned charm just to calm her down.

"I'm not used to women throwing themselves at me."

Oh my God, how corny! Did I really say that?

Elizabeth's a sweet girl, with an open face, although she's was a bit slow on the uptake. I'd always thought that women warm to a man with a sense of humour - I couldn't be sure that my witty barbs hit the target every time, though.

We must have spent at least an hour and a half in that freezing cold waiting room. Funny that; neither of us seemed to care. She was certainly pretty. I'd seen that look in a woman's eyes before and I know a winner when I see one. Obviously when I discovered that she was the daughter of Ben Railton, Chairman of Cannon's, I suddenly realised the potential.

I certainly get points for staying power. In the beginning Elizabeth's ex cast a shadow over everything, despite the fact she'd made it clear exactly where she stood.

Then things started to turn nasty. He was always around when he wasn't wanted. He tried to spread rumours about me but the other guys just laughed in his face. He's a bit of a brute. Quite frankly, I'd rather put up with having the aerial bent off my car than face pistols at dawn.

On top of all that, I've had to keep the whole thing quiet. All hell would break loose if Viv ever found out. You don't think Viv suspects anything, do you?

Come on, let's face it. I've been around a while and seen some action in that time. Anyone who's worked a summer season in a holiday camp soon gives up counting. But isn't it funny how you only remember the ones that got away?

I'm sick and tired of looking at those broken tiles. The damp in the corner is getting worse. Once it takes hold it's a devil of a job to get shot of it.

So, here I am, six months on, stuck in this mouldy dump with Viv. We decided to shack up temporarily, just to see how things would work out. It was fine at first, we took it in turns to cook and wash up but we always made a point of doing the weekly shop together. We even got on well with each other's friends.

Somewhere along the line it's turned sour - perhaps it happened too quickly? All we ever seem to do is argue nowadays. I've never been the jealous type but the more Viv accuses me the more I need to get away.

How much better I'll feel in that pristine dress shirt. I'll primp and prink my shirt cuffs through my freshly pressed suit. I'll set it all off with that matching silk bow tie. Then I'll really look the business.

Excuse me while I check the ring is definitely in my jacket. It'll be the fifth time I've checked tonight, won't it? Elizabeth will be delighted and when I propose it will seal our fate together. I'm in no doubt about that.

Oh my God, is that the front door? Surely it can't be Viv back so soon? I was going to leave a note but there's no time for alibis. I'm not in the mood for long explanations about what I do with my life and who I do it with. I'm going straight from now on.

Once Elizabeth has said yes I will tell Viv it's all over. Finished! Damn it! If that lazy slob's brought back fish and chips again, he'll just have to sit and eat it on his own...

When The Screaming Stops **

All I could hear was her screaming...

It all began with her bad dream. Rosemary would always wake up screaming. It was awful. I asked her what was wrong; it was that dream again. Whilst driving on the motorway we were suddenly enveloped in thick fog.

"Slow down," she said.

But I didn't listen; I was in too much of a hurry to get there. Apparently, there was a delay and a whole line of traffic was waiting to get through. We careered straight into the back of the lorry. I only had a slight cut; Rosemary can't remember anymore. I suppose that's the point where she wakes up screaming.....

So, I decided we should take a holiday. "Things have been getting on top of you - we both need a break," I told her.

We didn't really get off to a very good start. Rosemary was always reluctant to take any time off. Whilst we knew where we were heading, we couldn't agree how to get there.

"I'm all for a ride through the countryside," I enthused.

"No, we must take the motorway," she insisted.

Ah, well, she never was much of a map reader anyway. As it turned out, we had to pull off the motorway which was closed due to a nasty accident. So, we ended up on the scenic route after all.

God, it was dreadful; utter chaos. There were sirens wailing, flashing lights everywhere and policemen running all over the place. I remember seeing men rushing from an ambulance with a stretcher. I was glad to get away from it, I can tell you. It's not something I ever want to see again.

It seemed oddly quiet as we turned into the country lane. I felt a great sense of relief to be away from all that noise and confusion, but, at the same time, guilty that I should have been there to help. As the headlights picked out vague shapes in the mist ahead, I turned towards Rosemary. She seemed deep in thought.

"I think we're lost," she said eventually, her words hanging in the air. "I think we should turn back."

My heart sank: "No, come on, let's press on," I said, trying to sound encouraging. "I'm sure we'll come across a small village or something soon. We can always ask for directions there."

Just then, the fog seemed to lift. I clearly saw some farm buildings and we drove past a few cottages. Shortly, we arrived in the market place, and the warm lights from the shop windows seemed to beckon.

"Let's stop and have something to eat," I suggested. "I'm starving; do you fancy something?"

Rosemary shook her head. "Oh, come on, it'll do you good," I insisted.

But as I looked I saw that Rosemary was quite pale. Perhaps it was that accident. It must have upset her too.

We went to find the baker's tea room. The aroma of freshly baked bread and hot coffee wafted out to greet us. We chose a table tucked away in a corner. A pretty waitress dutifully took our order, jotting it all down on her little pad. I felt warm and safe. It was sanctuary after the drama we'd been through. I looked at Rosemary for some confirmation, but she seemed distant, which made me feel bad about dragging her in there. As I was about to speak, the waitress arrived with a pot of piping hot coffee and two Chelsea buns. I tucked in heartily. Rosemary didn't touch hers.

Just then, I thought I caught a glimpse of an old man standing by the window outside the tea room. His appearance seemed strangely familiar. If Rosemary saw him, she pretended not to. Suddenly, Rosemary got up as if to leave. I turned round in horror.

"No!" I pleaded, "Stay here with me."

She smiled and moved over towards the ladies room and I felt silly. Partly to hide my embarrassment, I went to settle the bill. As I was waiting to collect my change, I glanced over at the front door and saw Rosemary walking towards the

235

old man. I felt as though I would lose her and an icy fear seized me.

"Thank you for calling, sir," chimed the cashier, "I hope you enjoyed your meal."

"Yes...thank you," I stuttered, my attention distracted momentarily. When I received my change, I glanced back towards the doorway. Both Rosemary and the old man had disappeared.

"Where did they go?" I demanded.

"Who?" said the pretty waitress, puzzled.

"The old man and my wife," I cried. "You saw me with her earlier, don't you remember?"

She looked at me in disbelief: "No, I'm sorry sir. As I remember, you came in on your own."

There was no time to argue. I fled outside in pursuit of Rosemary. Night had fallen and thick fog had descended once more on the market place. As I stumbled around in the dim light, I heard the toll of a church bell in the distance. My heart was thumping as I made my way towards the sound. As it grew louder, I was desperate to find Rosemary.

As I reached the lych-gates, I could make out the figure of the old man standing at the threshold.

"What have you done with her?" I cried. "Give her back! I can't go on without her."

The old man stared back at me, unmoved. His eyes seemed to go forever.

"I couldn't help it, it wasn't my fault," I begged. "I didn't see the lorry until it was too late. It was thick fog you see. I tried to stop, but it was too late. Why her? Why not me?"

The old man turned his head slowly and I followed his gaze. In the graveyard, the moonlight picked out a tombstone and I saw Rosemary's name. The words seemed to glow and then gradually fade away. I felt the cold earth closing in around me.

I saw myself back at the motorway. The policemen were there and the lights were flashing but I felt calm. I was standing looking down at Rosemary. I could now feel my heart beating and was aware of my lungs breathing in the chill night air. Rosemary was still. She had died. She's gone.

I looked back but the old man had vanished. I turned and walked away from the churchyard. Then I noticed something. The screaming had stopped. I've finally accepted that life has to go on without her.

1st February '93

"When I glanced across the room again I saw that he was still watching me. I knew I had seen him before - somewhere."

I was reading an article, in the Bleson Times, because my editor had asked me to research violent deaths that had occurred in Bleson-on-sea. A young woman had given her account, at an inquest, on the death of a young man on 1st February 1893.

I found a picture of the young woman and ascertained that she was 23 years of age. It wasn't something I could explain at first but I knew her from somewhere. By coincidence, I thought, we had similar features and strangely enough she was also engaged to be married.

Her story was very intriguing, so much so, I was gripped by a relentless thirst for more information. The poor unfortunate young man's picture accompanied the article which stated that it was his 25th birthday when the accident had happened. She said at the inquest that she'd been aware of him staring at her, in the waiting room, at the local railway station.

"He looked nervous, lonely and lost. There was a glare of desperation in his eyes," she said. "At first I felt sorry for him but I began to feel uncomfortable with him staring at me. I decided to cancel my trip and I promptly left."

What happened next is none too clear. He'd apparently followed her to the cliff-top just outside the town. He hadn't got very close to her but he'd made her feel very nervous. She'd turned round to see him standing precariously on the cliff-edge.

"Go away," she cried, "leave me alone, you are frightening me."

He said nothing but just stood and stared at her. She panicked and started to scream. Then, suddenly, the cliff-edge gave way beneath his feet and he fell to his death.

"Maybe he had just wanted to talk," she said. "If I had not shouted the way I did, perhaps he would still be alive today."

I felt a personal sadness; I wished there was something I could have done to help. As it was the tragedy had tormented her for the rest of her life; she'd never quite got over it.

At the inquest it was learned that the young man was a farmer who had kept himself to himself. He wasn't an educated man but he had had a natural talent for art. One of his sketches was printed with the article. I compared his sketch to the picture of the young girl and I was amazed at the likeness.

I mentioned this story to the librarian. She said she was aware of the tragedy but believed it had happened in 1793 and not a hundred years later. She was very sure of her facts. A lonely young man had fallen to his death whilst pursuing an attractive young woman. I checked through the reference books and sure enough a similar incident had occurred in 1893 to that of 1793.

I decided to record both accidents for my files and I was immediately struck by the coincidences. The descriptions of both men and women were very similar.

The information that I'd recorded had sent a shiver up my spine. Each incident had happened on 1st February. Both young men had died on their 25th birthday. What really shook me was when I discovered that I shared the same birthday with both young women and, like me, they were aged 23. Subconsciously I glanced at today's newspaper. It was 1st February 1993.

I was convinced and my next course of action was clear. I prayed I wouldn't be too late as I made my way towards the cliff-top. A narrow sandy path led me to it and there stood before me was a young man near the edge of the cliff. I rushed towards him and grabbed hold of his arm.

"Come away from the edge," I shouted, "this time I must save you."

"Go away," he cried, "leave me alone, you are frightening me."

He managed to break free of my grip and took a few steps back. Then, suddenly, the earth crumbled beneath his feet and he fell to his death.

I've made my statement at the inquest and a verdict of accidental death has been recorded once again. My editor and my friends just say I'm suffering from the traumas of the accident. I'll get over it they tell me. But I know, deep in my heart, in 2093 I will be driven with the same curious desire to go to those cliffs once more. I just hope that what ever action I take will finally save the young man's life.

www.ingramcontent.com/pod-product-compliance
Lightning Source LLC
Chambersburg PA
CBHW012150260626
47155CB00020B/3550